Shifting Dreams

By JM Kline

Text Copyright © 2013 JM Kline

Cover Art Design Copyright © 2013 - 3CFMedia

ISBN-13: 978-1490524597
ISBN-10: 1490524592

All rights reserved. No part of this publication may be reproduced, stored in a retrieval system, or transmitted in any form or by any means – electronic, mechanical, photocopying, recording, or otherwise – without the prior written permission of the author. The only exception is brief quotations in published reviews.

For my husband. Thank you for putting up with my odd hours, frantic re-writes, and mid-sentence plotting. Special thanks to my girls for letting me sit down and write.

Chapter One

"What do you mean I'm a shape-shifter? Nice joke, guys." I stared at my parents – they were obviously nuts.

I couldn't believe they'd made me turn the TV off for this. I glanced at the clock on the BluRay player. I'd already missed half of my favorite show. I wondered how much longer they would keep this up.

"It's true, Tessa. You're a shape-shifter, just like the rest of us." Dad had his 'serious' face on, but I still wasn't convinced. They had to be teasing me. I rolled my eyes and crossed my arms in front of me. I leaned back in my chair and threw my legs over the armrest. If they were going to keep messing with me, I was going to get comfortable.

"Okay, fine. I'll play. I'm a shape-shifter. What do I 'shift' into?" I asked.

"Well, honey, that hasn't been determined yet," Mom said. "You won't change until you're seventeen, and nobody is quite sure why each of us has an affinity for one animal over another."

"That's right," Dad agreed. "With a few exceptions, kids rarely shift into the same thing as their parents."

"Wow. You guys seriously thought this one through." I turned to Mom. "Did you practice this or some-"

Mom was gone. In her chair perched a golden eagle.

"Mom!" I fell out of my chair and scrambled to stand up. "Dad, what happened to Mo-"

Dad wasn't in his chair, either. Of course not. Instead, there was a beaver. A friggin' beaver!

I ran. I ran out of the living room, up the stairs, into my bedroom, and slammed the door. What else could I do? My parents just turned into animals. Yep, that is what I saw. Animals. In my living room.

"Tessa?" Dad was on the other side of the door. "Tessa honey, open up. Your mom and I didn't mean to scare you. We just wanted you to know we aren't joking."

"I'll stay in here, thank you very much. There are no crazy animals in here." I heard Dad sigh and a minute later, he walked away.

I glanced at my bed and decided I needed to make it. I threw the purple and black cover over my pillows and fluffed it all around. I put my stuffed animals on the top of the bed. I took them off and threw them in the corner. I went over and set them all on my shelf, smallest to biggest. Then biggest to smallest.

What was I even doing?

I had to be in shock. I mean, how was I supposed to react to news like this? My parents tell me I'm a freak, from a family of freaks, and they expect me to just…what? Be cool with it? Yeah, right.

I opened my window and carefully climbed out. I had to talk to Chloe. Even my best friend in the world wouldn't believe this one.

I ran the couple of blocks to her house and quickly climbed the oak tree outside her window. The light was on, so I tapped the window three times, our signal.

Chloe was at the window in record time. "What took you so long, T?"

I stared at Chloe like she was crazy. She was wearing her usual black pants and shirt, but her curly red hair was even messier than its normal nest. Her green eyes were brighter than usual, and her skin was paler than its normal shade of white. "What do you mean? Was I supposed to come over tonight?"

"No, you idiot!" Chloe smacked my arm. "Your parents just had 'the talk' with you right? I can't believe it took you so long to get over here. We need a game plan!"

"Wait, 'the talk?' You mean your parents just told you what I am? Does the whole stupid town know that I'm a freak?" This was just getting better and better. I figured I was supposed to keep this thing secret, but apparently everyone gets to know. Even if she is my best friend, I didn't want Chloe to know I was a monster.

"Thanks. I'm a freak too, you know," she said and flung herself onto her bed.

I carefully moved aside the giant pile of clothes on the comforter – I loved her, but Chloe is not exactly neat – and sat down

"Wait, what? We're talking about the

same thing here, right?" She couldn't possibly be talking about what I was talking about. I mean…what were the odds?

"Yes, if we're talking about us being shape-shifters. Ugh. I can't believe I just said that. It sounds so weird. I'm a shape-shifter," she said. She scrunched her nose and brought her eyebrows together. She shook her head and her face cleared. She probably knew how stupid she looked when she did that.

"At least we're in it together," I gave her a half-hearted smile and lay in bed next to her. I stared up at the ceiling. "I wonder why they didn't tell us before."

"Dad said that the adults decided a long time ago not to tell us until we were heading into high school. As if we weren't all nervous enough, the whole class gets to learn about this the day before school starts." Chloe made a sound of disgust.

"Seriously? The whole school is like us?

It's bad enough this stupid town makes us stay in middle school through ninth grade, but now we find out we're going to Freak High!" I wanted to scream. How could they do this to me?

I sighed. I guess it could be worse. I could be going through all of this without my best friend.

"Freak High, where the school mascot doesn't need to wear a suit!" Chloe preferred to deal with crappy news with humor. I might as well play along.

"Where the class pet might eat you for dinner!"

We giggled for a minute, which quickly turned into a sound of pain. Like when I stub my toe and I have to laugh or else I'm going to cry. We stopped laughing and stared into space for a bit.

I couldn't stop thinking about what we were about to go through. I'm sure Chloe was thinking the same.

Besides, I didn't know what to say. I mean, what could I say? It's not like I could ever expect something like this to happen. Mom said they couldn't predict what I'd be. What if I turned into some crazy predator and ate my best friend? Oh, jeez…. "Chloe, no matter what happens, promise me nothing will change between us?"

She looked at me like I was the crazy one. "Of course, nothing will change. T, we've been friends for like, ever. I don't think anything could ever change that. Unless you ate me or something. Then I'd have to go all Drama Queen on you."

We both grinned. I hadn't felt the need to hold her hand since we were eight and we had to cross the street together. I grabbed her hand now, though. I needed my best friend.

After a few minutes, Chloe sighed and glanced at the clock. "You'd better go home. We have school tomorrow."

"Yay." I was not looking forward to it. "See you at the corner?"

"See you then." We hugged for a full minute. "T, let go. You need to leave."

I sighed and left. After I crawled back into my room, I collapsed into bed. My mind was racing. What was school going to be like? I'd imagined high school to be similar to middle school, only a lot harder. Now I had to wonder if I would walk in to class and see an ostrich. I had no idea what to expect.

A lot of my classmates got excited about the new werewolf movies and stuff, but I'd never been into that sort of thing. Now that seemed to be my life.

I pictured myself as a slobbering half-human monster and shuddered. Just because Mom and Dad looked like "normal" animals when they changed in front of me doesn't mean that I was going to be as lucky. What if I changed into some human-animal monster? Good luck trying to find someone who wants to date that!

I flopped to my side and stared at the door. My whole future had changed and I had no idea what I was in for.

That probably explained what happened after I fell asleep.

I noticed the dark first. Glancing around, I saw that I was in a cave. An eerie blue light emanated from the center, where a cluster of quartz jutted from the earth. The top was flat and almost smooth and came up to my knees.

As I walked toward the pedestal – I realized now that's what it was – I saw more details. I could see the ceiling, the same smooth red limestone that made up the foothills around my house. I looked down and saw I wore a white linen dress and no shoes. The stone felt cool on my feet. I heard a humming noise coming from all around me and searched beyond the reaches of the faint light.

Several sets of glowing eyes emerged from the dark. As my sight adjusted, small forms materialized. I saw my parents in their animal forms – a beaver and a golden eagle. Behind them were an owl and a deer. When I saw the bear, I knew I should be frightened, but seeing it actually made me feel better, maybe even safer.

I stepped up onto the pedestal and knelt in the center. My knees pressed into the rough quartz and I was grateful for the linen dress I wore, even if it was thin. I heard a shuffling, and my dad pressed his head against my hand. Feathers ruffled beside me and my mom leaned into my left side.

The humming got louder. The animals moved close to me, creating a circle. I noticed some smaller animals I hadn't seen earlier – a snake, a fox, a ferret, and a German Shepherd.

Suddenly, I felt a searing pain that began in my toes. It worked its way up through my body and exploded in my head. I cried out and the pain stopped as quickly as it started. I heard my dad's voice. *It's over sweetheart.* I slowly opened my eyes and looked around. The cave had gotten bigger. Or maybe...I looked down and saw my paws –

BEEP BEEP BEEP BEEP!

I shot up and smacked my alarm clock. Ugh. What a nightmare.

"Way to start off the school year," I muttered. Shaking the dream away, I got out of bed and took a shower. I brushed my long black hair up into its usual ponytail and pulled on my jeans.

I stood there for a minute and tried to decide what shirt to wear. *What did it matter?* If someone at Freak High wanted to make fun of me for a shirt, I'd just sic my own personal eagle on them. *Take that, little field mouse.* I pulled on a red shirt and slipped on my sandals. August in the Colorado foothills was still way too hot to wear shoes with socks.

Walking downstairs, I heard the sound of clattering pans in the kitchen. I hesitated. I hadn't seen my parents since they had turned into animals, and I didn't know how I was supposed to act.

"Good morning, Tessa!" Mom put a big plate of bacon on the table when I walked in. "You're here just in time. The first waffle is almost ready."

Obviously, Mom was going to ignore the fact that anything had ever happened. If she wanted to butter me up, I could live with that. Maybe being a shifter wouldn't be so bad if it came with waffles and bacon.

I'd just put the waffle on my plate when my 16-year-old brother, Tony, walked in. I knew for a fact that he had just been in the bathroom giving his brown hair that perfect 'just-rolled-out-of-bed' style. I also knew it took him about thirty minutes. He wore his red and gold high school football jersey. Go, Shadow Hills Rams!

"Hey, Squirt," he said as he plopped down next to me and reached over with his fork to grab my steaming-hot waffle.

He drenched my waffle with syrup and shoveled it into his mouth. I sighed. There was no point in arguing. He had already eaten half of it before I could even react. I grabbed some bacon, pulled my sketch pad from the bag at my feet, and drew a picture of Tony, falling off a cliff. His head was shaved and he was crying. Snot dripped out of his nose onto the waffle he was holding. *Ha. Take that.*

I had barely enough time to eat before I walked to the corner to meet Chloe.

She wore her favorite black jeans and a retro Van Halen shirt. Chloe wore a lot of black, but she didn't buy into the whole "depressed and angsty" thing. I think she did it because it bothered her dad, Shadow Hills' very own Sheriff. "Come on, T. We're going to be late."

We walked to school and found the class roster. We had homeroom together, which was great. We went to Mrs. Britten's room and chose seats in the middle. The back was already full. Go figure.

When the bell rang, a woman walked in. She was tall and slender. My hand itched to draw her as a giraffe. I could just imagine her already-long neck stretching until her blonde head hit the ceiling and her big 70's glasses fell off her face. I smiled at the image. This might not be so bad.

"Settle down class," she said. She waited until everyone stopped talking. "Thank you. Welcome to Shadow Hills High School. I am Mrs. Britten, and I will be your homeroom teacher this year. You will come to me every morning for attendance then you will have some quiet time to read or talk to me about homework from your other classes or any problems you may be experiencing.

"As you all know, this year marks an

Shifting Dreams

important change in your lives. I do hope you'll come to me with any concerns about the changes you will be going through, both metaphorically and literally. I know you all have a lot of questions, but we do not have time to answer them all today."

Mrs. Britten turned to her desk to grab a stack of small paperback books. She held one up.

"This is a guide book that will answer many of your questions. I will assign one to each of you today. Do not lose this book. It will be a valuable resource for you. If you do lose it, you will be fined and required to read the library copy, which does not leave the building. Are there any questions?"

Several kids raised their hands.

"Any questions that pertain solely to the use of this book?"

Every hand went down.

"Excellent." She walked around the

room and gave us each a book. *Shifters: A History.* I flipped through it. It was a small-ish version of a standard textbook. Oh, goody.

Before we left, we picked up our class schedules from the front of the room. U.S. History, Algebra, Biology. I didn't know what I was expecting, but these classes sounded downright normal. I thought this was Freak High. Where were the classes on how to sharpen your talons and catch a fish with your mouth?

I didn't have time to think about it. Time between classes was short. It seemed even shorter than normal, since I didn't have the slightest idea where I was going. I stared at my map, searching for room 217. I suddenly found myself sitting on the ground with a sore butt.

"So sorry about that," said a voice with a slight accent. I looked up and saw a fairly attractive boy. At least, he would be attractive if his brown hair was longer and his nose wasn't crooked. I'd never seen him before, which was unusual in a town the size of Shadow Hills.

He reached out his hand to help me up. "I was trying to find room 217. Do you know where it is?" He was a little timid and a lot lost.

"Not exactly, but that's where I'm headed." We went to the next hallway and I searched. "According to the map, there should be a short hallway over here." I heard him follow me. What was that saying? 'The blind, leading the blind?'

"My name is Vin," he said. "My family just moved here."

"Hi, I'm Tessa," I said. "Ooh! I found it!"

Room 217 was off to the right at the end of the hallway kind of shoved a few feet back in between the rows of lockers. It was obviously designed to confuse kids on their first day. We walked in just in time for the bell to ring.

"Take your seats, everyone. I am Mr. Rogers, and this is U.S. History." His dark eyes darted around the classroom. Someone dropped a backpack and he cringed.

After he passed out a syllabus, he droned on about what was on it. I let my mind wander a bit. I was staring at the wall for several seconds before I realized that Mr. Rogers was no longer there. I blinked.

All the students laughed. I glanced at the floor, where a couple of kids were pointing. I blinked again. Sitting in front of Mr. Rogers' desk was a turtle, curled up inside its shell. As I watched, the air around the turtle became fuzzy and then Mr. Rogers reappeared in its place.

"Okay, who threw that spit wad?"

Chapter Two

Mr. Rogers was mad. He glared around the classroom, which made everyone stop laughing quickly. His gaze stopped on Westy, the captain of the JV football team. "Arthur Weston," he said. "Any relation to Mike?"

Westy shrugged. "Sure."

"Did he put you up to this?" Mr. Rogers' face was super red by now.

"I don't know what you're talking about, sir." His smirk told a different story.

Mr. Rogers' eyes narrowed even more. "I'll be watching you."

Westy shrugged again and Mr. Rogers went back to being boring for another thirty-two minutes. The bell finally rang and we gathered our things. Vin followed me out of class.

"What do you have next?" He pulled out his schedule and peeked over my shoulder at mine.

"Algebra. 219 – right across the hall. Sweet." There are no words to describe how happy that made me.

"Oh. Me, too." We walked across the hall and sat down. I saved a seat for Chloe.

"Hey, Tessa. What's up?" Chloe sat down when she came in and looked questioningly at Vin.

"Hey, Chlo. This is Vin. He just moved here from…where did you used to live?"

Vin shrugged."We've been everywhere. Just moved from California. But we lived for a couple of years in the Brazilian rain forest. I mostly grew up all around Australia." Ah-ha! That explained the accent.

"Wow, that sounds like fun. So

uhm…what are you guys doing here in Shadow Hills?" Chloe sounded weird.

"My parents heard this was a good shifter community," he said.

Chloe visibly relaxed at this. She must have been wondering if he was somehow the only non-shifter in the town.

"They wanted to be sure I was 'comfortably ensconced in a community where I could grow to my full potential.'" Vin's mocking tone told me that he was quoting his parents.

"Oh, okay. Considering we all just found out about this, I guess now is as good a time as any to be the new kid."

He frowned. "Yeah, I don't get that. Why didn't you all know about it already? I've known since forever. My parents were never shy about changing in front of me."

The teacher stood up and clapped. Apparently class was starting, so we couldn't talk anymore. I yawned. Algebra is just the most fascinating thing in the world. Which is why I decided to doodle in my notebook instead of listening.

I drew a boy's face. He had a square jaw and a sharp nose. His thin lips stretched into a small smile and his eyes crinkled in the corners. His eyes – I don't know where I got the inspiration for those eyes, but they had to be some of my best work. They were ringed with a darker color, almost fully shaded. There was a starburst pattern surrounding the pupil. They almost sparkled from the page. I wondered what color they would be.

The bell rang and I shoved my notebook in my bag. Finally, it was lunch time. I led the way outside. I saw an awesome tree this morning and thought it would be a great spot for lunch. Vin followed Chloe and me. It seemed we had made a new friend. I smiled.

We ate lunch and I told Chloe about what happened in U.S. History with the spit wad. She practically choked on her lunch, she laughed so hard. "A turtle? Really? That's hilarious! I wish I could have been there." She leaned forward and poked my knee. "See? This whole thing can't be all bad if we can have some fun with it."

"I'm excited to find out what I'm going to be," Vin said. He pulled a bag of chips out of his backpack and ate while talking. "I've done so much field research on different animals in the wild, but I can't imagine what I'll be. My parents thought I would have more options available if I studied more animals. I don't know if that's true, but I guess it can't hurt." He shrugged.

"There were some animals in the rain forest that I definitely do not want to change into." He shoved a handful of chips into his mouth and shuddered. "I had some close calls with poisoned spikes and sharp teeth when we were scouting for wildlife. Mom said that whenever shifters change into those kinds of things, they usually act like some kind of military for us. Poisoned weapons come in useful sometimes."

He leaned in close, and spoke in almost a whisper. "And then there are the abilities-" He grinned and upended the bag of chips into his mouth.

I looked at Chloe, then back at him, confused. "What are you talking about?"

He leaned back and shrugged, grabbing a bag of sandwiches. "Just the other cool things we might be able to do, besides changing. My dad's a tracker. Mom's a seeker. I've never really understood the difference, but they swear there is one."

"Still don't know what you're talking about." Chloe threw a grape. "Are you teasing us because we have no clue what's going on?"

Vin held his hands up in surrender. "No, I swear! We're all going to have some weird extra ability. I just hope mine isn't too weird."

Shifting Dreams

"Wait, you're serious?" That concerned me. What other secrets were my parents not telling me? "That sucks."

"It's probably not all that bad." Chloe ruined my pout. "It's like what happened this morning with the spit wad. I bet we can have fun with whatever gets thrown our way." She bit into her sandwich with delight. For someone who dressed so gothic all the time, she sure had a positive outlook on life.

Deciding to let this new information go for now, I went back to the original subject. "I just don't know about this whole thing. I mean, I have plans. I don't want to stay in this Podunk town forever. I want to go to Paris and be an artist. I know it's cliché, but it's what I want," I said.

Ever since I was four and I saw a picture of the Eifel Tower, I've wanted to see it. As I got older, I found out more and more about the city and all the other places in Europe and decided there was no other option – I had to travel the world.

Chloe nodded in agreement. We'd had this conversation before. I wanted to travel and she wanted to change the world. If we couldn't dream big, what's the point?

"You're an artist?" Vin perked up. "Can I see some of your stuff?"

I handed him my notebook. My parents bought it new for this school year, but it was already almost half-full with drawings at different levels of completion.

"These are great." Vin flipped through to the end, to my drawing from algebra. "Who is this?"

I took the book back. "I don't know. I was just doodling." I didn't know who the boy was, or why I drew him, but I felt protective of that sketch. I shoved it in my backpack and zipped it closed.

"There's nothing stopping you from living your dream," Vin said. "Nobody ever said you had to live in a shifter community forever. It's just nice to have other people you can talk to about things."

"I don't know if I want this. I mean, it's been suddenly sprung on me that I'm going to sprout fur and a tail, or something worse. Do I even have a choice in the matter?"

"Not really. From what I've been told, we change no matter what. The more shifters we have around us on our seventeenth birthday, the less painful it's supposed to be. There are stories about shifters who weren't around other shifters on their birthday, and they went crazy from the epic pain of the change."

"That's reassuring," Chloe said with a shudder. She grabbed her bag and stood. "It's almost time for next period. We should go."

We checked our schedules and discovered we shared most of our classes for the afternoon, including the last period when we all had a class called Life Skills.

The rest of the day went how I always expected high school to be. When we walked into Life Skills last hour, the teacher was sitting at his desk. He was nerdy, balding, and his glasses were practically hanging off his pointy nose. His clothes hung loosely around his skinny body. *Did the store not have clothes that fit?*

When the bell rang, he stood up and cleared his throat a few times. Nobody stopped talking. He struck before I could even register what happened. His hands were full of mp3 players and cell phones, taken mid-text. That shut everyone up. He set everything on the corner of his desk. "Welcome to Life Skills. Here, you will learn a great many things that will help you throughout life. Lesson one: pay attention to all the sounds and changes in your environment. Your attention to detail may be the difference between life and death.

"I am Mr. Norris. Now, who can tell me what just happened?"

I thought through what had happened

before I raised my hand.

"Yes, Miss...?"

"Tessa Brooks, sir." I figured I should be respectful of this teacher. He didn't look like much, but the trick he'd just pulled made me cautious. "You cleared your throat. Everyone kept talking and stuff, so you jumped over to the front few seats and took their things and jumped back to where you were. It was fast, but I think that's what happened...sir."

Mr. Norris nodded. "Very good, Tessa. That's exactly what happened. Did anyone else see this, now that Tessa has explained?"

I glanced around. Everyone was staring at me. I sank in my seat. Apparently I got to be a bigger weirdo than anyone else in Freak High. On the first day of school, no less. *Fantastic.*

Mr. Norris dropped a textbook on someone's desk, ending the Tessa Stare-Down. "This week's assignment will be to work in groups. Choose a place that is unfamiliar to all of you and sit and observe. Write down your observations, and then share with the rest of your group. Please do not cheat. You will not be graded on the similarities of your answers, just on whether you have done the assignment. The purpose of this exercise is to determine what your strengths already are when observing your surroundings." He dropped the last book off and went back to his desk. "Are there any questions?

"Great. Turn to page twelve." He spent the rest of the period going over the types of observations we could make. He talked about all the senses – sight, smell, taste, sound, touch. He even discussed intuition, which I thought was baloney. I escaped as fast as I could after class let out. Chloe and Vin caught up with me next to my locker.

"T, that was cool! How did you see all that?" Chloe's eyes were so big I thought her eyeballs might fall out.

"Seriously, Tessa. That was neat." Vin seemed impressed. "How did you do that?"

Shifting Dreams

I didn't know what they were so worked up about. It's not like I did anything all that special. I grabbed the huge stack of books I'd acquired that day and blew out a breath. "I've always seen things. Maybe it's because of my drawing or something. Mom always said I could see a field mouse in a haystack."

"Isn't the saying 'a needle in a haystack?'" Vin asked.

"Not for my mom." I shut my locker. "Come on. Let's go grab some ice cream and figure out where we're going to go for homework."

Chloe and I turned toward the door. I noticed Vin wasn't with us. I turned around and saw his back. "Vin? You coming?"

He turned around. "Oh, you meant me too? Sure!" He bounded over, reminding me of an over-eager puppy.

I decided I wouldn't mention his blush or the grateful smile he tried to hide. I liked him well enough, and I was pretty sure Chloe liked him too. I had to at least give him a chance. Being the new kid has got to suck.

Vin bought us ice cream and agreed that the forest just outside of town might be a good spot to go. None of us wanted to rush into our first assignment, so we figured we'd head over there after school on Friday.

I went to bed that night thinking about my day and how it was normal compared to what I was expecting. The classes were just normal classes. For the most part, the teachers were just normal teachers. Closing my eyes on a huge yawn, I figured this whole thing wasn't going to be so bad after all.

I was flying. No, it wasn't me. I felt the cool wind on my face, and I could feel a sensation of wind ruffling feathers, but they weren't mine. I was with someone. We peered below us and saw the forest near town. We swooped down for a closer look. There were three kids there, two girls and a boy. They weren't talking, just sitting against some trees with pencils in their hands. No longer interested, we flew back up and circled the town. There was a lot of noise coming from the football field.

The boys in red ran out on the field and lined up. Number 17 crouched over the football. He snapped it back and went head-to-head with a larger boy in green. He fell and his legs went out from under him. The other kid's foot landed directly on his ankle and we heard the crack. The boy in green got up. Number 17 didn't. He laid there and held his ankle with both hands.

We heard a whistle blow and flew up. None of this concerned us. We were free in the sky. Freer than we had ever been before. We knew we would have to come down eventually, but right now this was it. It was good to finally be seventeen.

"Tessa! Get your lazy butt out of bed! Mom says you're going to be late!" Tony pounded on my door.

"Go away, Tony, I'm up!" I yelled as I threw back the covers. I sat up and got dizzy. I guess that was to be expected from a flying dream. I got myself ready for school and headed out.

Classes for the rest of the week were the same as the first day, only more boring. No shifting teachers, no super-fast reflexes. Nada. So much for Freak High being more exciting than other schools.

Chapter Three

I met up with Chloe and Vin after school on Friday and we walked to the forest. Shadow Hills wasn't a big town, so it wasn't a big deal that none of us could drive yet.

We found a clearing just off the main path. We threw down our bags and sat in a circle against some trees. When I got settled, I saw that Vin had a box of snack cakes. He'd already eaten three and was in the middle of unwrapping another.

"Jeez, Vin," I said. "They're not going anywhere."

Vin grinned, but kept shoveling cakes into his mouth. I would never understand how boys can eat like that and still be so skinny. If I ate like that…well, I wouldn't even try. Opening my notebook, I drew a quick sketch of Vin, his mouth overflowing with snack cakes.

I sighed and looked around. The trees here were tall and there was very little undergrowth. A little bush off to the right of where Chloe sat had little berries. Some were scattered throughout the branches and some were half-eaten and scattered on the ground below it. I spent the next few minutes sketching the clearing, Chloe leaning forward over her notebook, Vin, cheeks full of food, writing in his. Then I decided to use some other senses. I closed my eyes and listened.

The wind blew through an aspen tree that I couldn't see. I could tell it was an aspen tree by the click-clacking of the leaves. I'd always thought it sounded like running water. A small chirp let me know there was a bird somewhere above us.

I inhaled and smelled the pine needles, the thick, rich scent of tree sap. There was an earthy undertone that told me there were mushrooms somewhere close.

A scratching noise made me open my eyes to peek. A family of rabbits had decided we were no threat and came out of their burrow. They nibbled on the berries near the bush. There was a movement behind them and I scanned up and saw a wolf.

I froze. I glanced behind it and caught glimpses of two more wolves. I made a squeak to alert Vin and Chloe of the danger.

"Chloe, stand up slowly," I heard Vin say. "Turn around and back up towards me." We all stood up and Chloe backed towards us. We stood together on the opposite side of the clearing.

"Now, let's all back up and-"

The wolf sat down and pawed at the air. I didn't know what it was doing.

Apparently Vin did. He let out a nervous laugh. "No problem, guys. They're not going to hurt us. Chloe, go ahead and get your bag and let's head out."

Chloe didn't move. She stared wide-eyed at the wolves. The other two had come out into the open. The leader was still sitting. It was large, with black fur, blue eyes, and a black muzzle. The one on the right was a silvery grey with patches of white on its tail and face, like a dog going white with age. The third one was slightly smaller than the other two. It had a light brown coat – almost golden. Its muzzle was a lighter gold color and its eyes were light, green maybe.

"Tessa, you're going to need to get Chloe's bag. I don't think they want me to come any closer," Vin said. "Please."

Glancing at Vin, I saw that he was backing Chloe up behind him. So much for 'they're not going to hurt us.' I moved forward, inch by inch. The wolves didn't react at all. I got about a foot away from the bag when the lead wolf lay down on the ground, as if to show me that he wasn't going to attack.

Shifting Dreams

I reached the bag and realized it was almost directly in front of the golden wolf. I tried not to make eye contact, but I couldn't help it.

Its eyes were the most brilliant green I had ever seen. I was close enough to see the emerald ring along the outside. The pupils were lined with a bright green that exploded into a firework pattern that was scattered with flecks of gold. They seemed familiar, but there was no way that was possible. I'd remember those eyes on an animal.

I snatched Chloe's bag and slowly backed up to where Vin and Chloe stood. Apparently, Chloe had recovered, because she quickly took her bag from my hands. We all backed away until we couldn't see the wolves anymore. Then, we turned around and ran.

We ran until we reached Chloe's house. We collapsed in her back yard, under the tree house we used to play in. I caught my breath first. "Vin, you have to explain what just happened."

"We met," Vin said, still out of breath, "our first wolf shifters."

"Oh," I said. I felt silly now for running away. I had only seen my parents and a teacher, but none of them were nearly as scary as the wolves.

"I guess we were in their territory. We can't go back there. We'll need to figure out somewhere else to do our assignment."

"Why can't we go back? They're shifters like us. You said yourself that they wouldn't hurt us." I was confused.

"They wouldn't hurt us this time. If we went back into their territory, knowing it's theirs…we can't take the chance." Vin had recovered his breath. "See, wolves are different than the rest of us. Nobody knows why, but wolf shifters always have kids that turn into wolves. Wolves don't mix with other shifters. We stay out of their way, and they stay out of ours."

I didn't understand but, of the three of us, Vin was the definitive expert on all things shifter, so I left it at that. Then I remembered something. "Why did *I* have to get the backpack? Why did you say they didn't want you any closer?"

Vin looked down at his hands. "Wolves are very territorial. Since I'm a guy, they see me as a threat. If I had gotten closer to them, they would have taken it as a threat and attacked...probably."

"You risked my life on 'probably?'" Jerk.

"Look, my parents told me everything I know. I'm just telling you what they told me."

I thought about what had happened. The green eyes of the golden wolf were so familiar – they're not the kind of eyes you forget. Now that I knew they were shifters, I knew it was possible I had met the person before. I just couldn't place him. I shrugged. No use worrying about it. If wolves really do keep to themselves, I wasn't ever going to have to remember.

Ultimately, we decided to use Chloe's back yard for our homework. Mr. Norris would never know. We hung out for a half an hour, writing things in our notebooks. When we compared, we found out that we each had very different strengths.

Vin's notes were about what he could feel – the wind, an ant running over his hand. It made us laugh when he discovered that the constant tickling he felt on his neck was one of Chloe's hairs that had gotten on his shirt. He also said he felt like we were being watched. But none of us saw anyone, so we figured he was just being self-conscious.

Chloe's observations were mostly about smells. She smelled her neighbor's freshly cut grass and Vin's cologne. She knew that Vin had been sneaking snack cakes when we weren't watching, and he wiped the telltale crumbs from his chin.

Shifting Dreams

I spent my time lying on my stomach drawing the patch of grass in front of my notepad. Some of the dirt peeked through, and the grass was in desperate need of mowing. A ladybug had crawled up a blade of grass and flown away, and a spider walked across the dirt, leaving a thin cord of webbing in its path.

We figured that was good enough for homework, so Vin and I left and went home. When I walked in the door, the house was silent. I knew Mom was still at work, but Dad is normally home by now. I checked the calendar on the fridge.

Tony-football-4:00.

I glanced at the clock. 4:42. I had time to eat some of Mom's chocolate chip cookies before anyone got home.

Munching away, I did the rest of my homework. After I finished, I checked the time. 6:15. Mom was usually home by six o'clock. I called her cell phone and got her voicemail. I was just about to leave a message when the front door opened.

I walked into the living room and saw Mom, followed by Tony and Dad. Tony was on crutches and wearing a cast on his leg. "What happened?"

"It was dirty playing, is what it was!" Dad was fired up. "That other player was on steroids or something! He looked like he was in his twenties!"

Tony sat down and rolled his eyes. "Dad, he's a second year senior. What do you expect?"

Mom put down her purse and came over. "It's just a fracture, nothing to worry about. Thank goodness Tony is turning seventeen next weekend, or he would have to wear this cast for at least six weeks."

Mom was a doctor. She had a practice in town, where she and one other doctor worked. It was kind of nice knowing we got preferential treatment whenever we got hurt.

"Oh," I said like I understood. I didn't. "Why would that make a difference? Oh, and sorry about your ankle, Tony. If you weren't such a wuss, you wouldn't have gotten hurt." I made a face at my brother and he glared back.

"Mom, can you make the little brat go away? Also, I think I deserve some ice cream for all my pain and suffering tonight." He threw the recliner back and closed his eyes. What a Drama Queen.

"That's enough, kids." Mom turned to me. "Tessa, when Tony shifts on his birthday, his bone will heal. A fracture is minor for us, so he shouldn't have any problems with it." With a smile, Mom went into the kitchen to make dinner. I heard her open the freezer. She was getting Tony some ice cream. This was so not fair.

"Tessa, honey, can you grab Tony's gym bag from the car?" Dad asked as he went into the kitchen.

"Ugh!" I stomped out to the car and pulled the bag out of the trunk. Tony's jersey fell out and I picked it up. Number 17. *Wait a minute…there was no way.* It had to be a coincidence. Football was a dangerous sport. People get hurt all the time.

I went inside and threw Tony's bag on his lap, making him jump. He opened his mouth to whine to Mom and I interrupted him. "Oops! Sorry. I didn't see you there," I said, running out of the room.

The memory of the dream I'd had this morning chased me up the stairs. There was no way it had anything to do with Tony getting hurt. Right?

I shook my head and felt a headache creep up the back of my neck. Great. I yelled down to Mom that I was going to bed early to get rid of my headache.

Tony glowered up the stairs and made a

face at me. "Sure, you've got a headache. You don't always have to be the center of attention, you know." He turned around and yelled to the kitchen. "Mom, is my ice cream ready yet?"

I rolled my eyes and got ready for bed. My head was pounding by the time my head hit the pillow, but I drifted right off to sleep.

***

I woke up Saturday feeling tired, but when I saw that it was noon, I figured I should get up. Mom and Dad both worked on Saturdays, but Mom would be calling to check on us soon and it wouldn't be good for me to sound like I just woke up. I'd learned that the hard way over the summer. I'm sure she was just jealous that she couldn't sleep late, but the punishment was bad enough that I didn't want to push it. Cleaning Dad's part of the bathroom was disgusting enough I only needed to do it once.

I ate breakfast in my pj's and flipped

through channels on the living room big screen. Five hundred channels and nothing on.

Deciding to see Mom at the clinic, and maybe get some chocolaty snacks from her receptionist, Doris, I took a shower and threw on some shorts and a tank top. Tony's bedroom door was still closed, so I decided not to wake him up. He could still clean a bathroom with a bum leg.

I grabbed my backpack so I could pretend to be doing homework if Mom asked, and headed out. The temperature had reached its high for the day, so my walk downtown wasn't terribly pleasant. I was glad to open the clinic door to a blast of cool air.

The smell of hospital antiseptic had never bothered me. I'd grown up with it, and it always seemed like my mom's special smell. Dad's was fresh-cut wood. I didn't get to visit his worksites often, but he usually came home with sawdust all over and the smell always made me think of him.

Shifting Dreams

Doris was sitting behind the counter, frowning at a dark computer screen.

"Hi, Miss Doris! What's up?"

Her head snapped around to look at me. Her grey bun didn't move an inch. I always wondered how she managed to get through every day with petrified hair on her head. She looked relieved when she saw it was me. "Oh, dearie. Thank goodness, you're here. This blasted machine, pardon my French, stopped working and I can't figure out what happened."

I smiled at Doris's "French" and walked over to check out the computer. Mom had bought it for Doris five years ago, thinking she was doing something nice and helping Doris become more efficient with appointments and files and whatever else she does. Doris always seemed to give it the "deer in the headlights" look. I don't know why Mom never saw it, but Doris got in the habit of asking me to fix whatever she did to the thing because she didn't want to appear ungrateful.

I searched around and turned the power strip behind the desk back on, pushing it further behind the tower so it couldn't be kicked off again. "All fixed," I said, grinning.

Doris was the sweetest old lady ever. My mom's parents lived in Italy or France or something, and we only visited my Dad's parents in Florida over Christmas break, so I'd always thought of Doris as my surrogate grandmother. She didn't seem to mind.

She smiled back and whispered, "There's some ice cream in the fridge. It'd be a shame for it to go to waste." She patted her thin belly and winked. She didn't fool me. She bought this stuff for me. And I loved her for it.

I walked into the small kitchen and heard Doris roll back to her desk, turn the computer on, and start mumbling. She'd probably need me again soon, but the chocolate beckoned from the freezer. Mint Chocolate Dream. Good stuff.

Shifting Dreams

Plopping down on a chair, I dropped my backpack beside me and decided to do some reading while I ate lunch. Technically, I hadn't had breakfast. But since it was after noon, I was going to call it lunch. Sweet, chocolaty, melty lunch.

I pulled out the book Mrs. Britten had given us, *Shifters: A History*. Still looked about as thrilling as it did when she'd handed them out. I glanced over the table of contents and something caught my eye. *Abilities, Traits, Levels.* I remembered the conversation with Vin and figured it was as good a time as any to find out what he meant.

*A shifter's abilities are not usually limited to changing form. Most shifters have latent abilities which allow them further benefit. These abilities are called **traits**. Traits are described as extra-sensory or instinctual abilities beyond that of a human's.*

"Well, it seems Vin wasn't wrong," I murmured under my breath. Taking another bite,

I let the chocolate melt in my mouth and leaned forward.

Traits are generally divided into three levels of aptitude. Level 1 traits are initially limited to one's animal form, though through practice can usually be extended to one's human form. These traits usually enhance one's senses, such as sub-or super-sonic hearing, strong olfaction, and vision enhancements.

Why someone would practice being a weirdo was completely alien to me. Changing into an animal was bad enough, why would someone want to be able to hear gossip from the next room? Wait, on second thought, that didn't sound too bad. I shrugged and kept reading.

Level 2 traits are innate sensory abilities, such as the ones described above, but can also enhance certain aspects of memory.

Memory? I had to talk to someone. I glanced through the doorway and saw Doris shaking her mouse. I wasn't sure what she was trying to do, but she probably wouldn't mind a distraction. I grabbed the book and went over to her desk, plopping down on her guest chair.

"Miss Doris," I pleaded. "Can you help me understand some of my homework?"

She gently set the mouse down and smiled, obviously grateful I'd come to her rescue. "Of course, dearie. What can I help you with?"

I opened the book and pointed to the section I was reading. "This is talking about abilities, and I just don't understand what it means. This part here," I pointed, "says that they enhance senses.

"I get that part, but this part here," I pointed again, "says something about enhanced memory? What's up with that?"

Silence distracted me from the passages I'd been reading, drawing my gaze up. Doris stared at me, eyes wide, sweat beading on her upper lip.

"What's wrong? Did I say something wrong?" Oh, no. Was this one of those things you don't talk about? Like when I'd gotten in trouble when I was little because I asked my mom why Mr. Gunner at the grocery store had no legs? Doris was the last person I'd wanted to offend.

Shaking her head quickly, she let out a breath. "No dearie, you're just fine asking these questions. It has just been so long since anyone has asked me about these things."

She patted my knee and I relaxed. "Our abilities are not generally discussed with those outside our own family. It's like family medical history, we share the information whenever we're ill or not able to do things that we used to, and we leave it at that." She smiled at me and leaned back in her chair. "It's a good thing I consider you family, dearie."

"Thank you, Miss Doris. I'm sorry. I didn't know it was a hot topic." I sat there, trying to figure out a way I could let her out of this conversation. She obviously didn't want to talk about it.

Mom walked out of the patient room just then and came over, smiling. "Hi, sweetheart. What are you girls discussing?"

Doris breathed a sigh of relief, and I took the opportunity to transfer the heat to Mom. "We were talking about abilities. I just read about them in my book and I don't understand what it's all about."

Mom's smile got even wider, and I knew I was in for a long lecture about the medical reasoning behind this and that. *Oh, goody.* "Let's go into my office. I don't have any appointments for a while."

Following her into the office, I sat in front of her desk and stared at her until she settled into her giant office chair and started talking. "I'd love to lecture you about everything I know about traits and ability levels, but why don't you go ahead and ask me what you want to know?"

I breathed a sigh of relief. Mom's lectures could be brutal, and I was so glad she finally figured that out. I put aside all of my initial questions and blurted out the first thing that I wanted to know. "What can you do?"

Mom laughed, and leaned back. "I am what is called a 'medivoyant.' I can tell what is making a person sick or hurt just by looking at them. Of course, I had to go to school so I could be qualified to fix them, but it does make diagnosing a medical condition much easier."

I let this process for a minute. It explained why Tony could never get away with pretending to be too sick to go to school. It also explained why she never took our temperature when we were running a fever. She'd always known when we were coming down with something, and made us pop a bunch of vitamins and supplements so we wouldn't be sick for long.

"Huh. Okay, well that explains a lot." I considered that for a minute. "What about Dad?"

"Your dad has a variation of spatial intuition that allows him to see issues when he's on a job site. He can basically see if a beam is not going to hold, or if any structure is unsound. It's why he went into construction instead of architecture."

Sweet. "Are all of these trait thingies as cool as what you guys have?"

Mom smiled. "There are very few traits that are not useful for some kind of career. How strong the ability is in each trait helps us determine what we're going to do with it when we've grown."

"Wait, are you saying I don't have a choice about what I'm going to be when I grow up? That's not fair!" I pouted.

Mom shook her head. "Not everyone has a trait that they wish to use for their job, however most of us use them in one way or another. You can still do whatever you want. Paris is still waiting for you, Tessa. Don't worry about that."

Her assurance made me feel better, and I glanced down at my book. "Okay, so what about these ability levels? What do they mean? Do people with the level one abilities get treated like poop while everyone else runs around being medivoyant and whatever else?"

"Not at all. Your dad is actually considered a level one intuitive. He can see when something has been done wrong, but he doesn't know until it's completed.

"Level two intuitions allow a person to see when something is happening while it's going on. That's what I do. While I'm sure there are some shifters who feel they're better than others because of a level three status, I've never met any."

"What about level three?" I glanced down at my book.

Shifting Dreams

Level 3 traits are rare, and include manipulation of external forces and psychic abilities. "Psychic abilities? That has to be a misprint, right?"

I gave my mom a funny look, but she shook her head. "No, that's correct. It's a very rare ability. I've never met anyone who had level three abilities except during college." She sat back and smiled. "Gary Long could make grass grow. He could affect other plants, but he enjoyed growing grass. He is a landscape artist nowadays."

Considering that was supposed to be some super-cool ability, it was actually kind of lame. I wasn't so worried anymore about probably getting a level one trait, as long as it wasn't something so dumb.

"Is there anything else you want to know, sweetheart?" Mom leaned forward, and I could tell she was ready to keep going. Unfortunately for her, I was done. She'd given me all the answers I wanted.

"No, I think that's it." I saw her frown in response and added, "For now. Thanks, Mom!" I walked away, book in hand. She'd given me a lot to think about. Not only was I going to sprout feathers or fur, I would also be gaining some new ability. And of course, I didn't know what to expect with either one.

On one hand, it was a good thing I had a couple of years to process before it all happened. On the other, I kind of wished I didn't have two years to stress and worry about it.

Chapter Four

Sunday morning was usually pretty lazy for all of us. Even Mom slept in, if you can call waking up at nine sleeping in. I rolled out of bed at eleven, groggy and hungry.

When I went down to the kitchen, Dad peered over his newspaper at me. "Good morning, sport. Your mom picked up some of that sugary cereal you like so much. Better eat some before Tony sees it."

"Thanks, Dad." I smiled and grabbed the CinnaPops from the cupboard. I figured I could probably hide it behind the box of oatmeal packets for a couple of days before Tony ate his way through the cabinet and found it.

While I munched, I thought about my day. I had some homework to do. As much as I *loved* algebra, I figured I'd skip it for today. I remembered there was a new romcom out, so I pulled out my phone and sent Chloe a text. *Wanna go C that new chickflick today?*

I didn't have long to wait before she responded. *YES! Get me out of the house. Let's do the mall cineplex and pick up some churros.*

I made a face. I totally didn't understand Chloe's love of churros. Something about all that cinnamon made me want to sneeze. But, if that's what it took to get out of the house...*Sure. C U in an hour.*

"Dad, can I have twenty bucks to go see a movie with Chloe?" I gave him my best puppy dog eyes, but I knew he would say yes.

He smiled and bopped my nose before reaching into his pocket for his wallet. "Sure, honey. Don't spoil your dinner by eating too much popcorn, okay?"

I grabbed the cash and leaned over to kiss his cheek. "I promise," I said while throwing my cereal bowl in the dishwasher.

I ran up to my room and took a quick

shower. I examined my closet thoroughly before picking out a pair of jean shorts that made my legs look long, and a purple striped t-shirt. I absolutely love purple. It highlighted how dark my hair was, and was great with my skin tone.

I slipped on my favorite sandals and practically skipped out the door. I walked over to Chloe's house, which was on the way to the mall. It wasn't much of a mall, more of a shopping center. It was all outdoors, with two strips of shops and a 12-screen theatre at the end, making it a U-shape.

Chloe was waiting out front for me when I got to her house, and we walked together to the theater. On the way there, I told her about my conversation with my mom.

"So your mom can just look at you and, BAM! She knows what's wrong with you?" She grinned. "Wicked cool. I wonder what my parents can do. With everything else going on, I totally forgot about what Vin said. I'm surprised you did homework without having to. You feeling okay?"

She tried to put her hand on my forehead, but I swatted it away. "I'm fine. Besides, me doing homework yesterday meant I could go out today, so don't knock it."

"Bet you didn't do your math, though." I didn't say a word, but she grinned. She knew me too well.

"Whatever, okay!" We'd reached the mall. "Let's get our tickets and some snacks."

Chloe snuck her churro into the movie and I crunched on popcorn. The movie was exactly what we both hoped it would be. A story about true love and half-naked hotties.

We walked home after and I realized it had been an almost normal Sunday. I went to bed that night hoping that 'normal' would continue.

We were in the back yard. Mom, Dad and Tony were all there. Chloe was there talking to her parents.

I saw Vin with two other adults. They looked a lot like Vin, so I figured they must be his parents. There were several teachers from school and a couple of adults I didn't know. Something caught their attention, and I turned to see what it was.

Tony was...shimmering. I had no other way to describe it. His face twisted into a grimace of pain. He held onto Mom's hand and I could tell he was squeezing because her face crunched in pain.

Dad was replaced by a beaver and several other adults in the yard suddenly changed into animals and ran toward Tony, who was still shimmering.

"Don't fight it, Anthony," said Mom. "Just let go."

I didn't know if Tony was listening or if he just gave up trying to control what was happening, but he stopped shimmering. My brother was no longer sitting in the chair. Next to the table sat a brown bear. It stood up on all fours and shook like a dog after a bath. Then it stood on its back legs and yelled. It rolled around the yard a couple of times before it stopped and looked at Mom.

She smiled at it, tears rolling down her face. "I'm so proud of you, Anthony. Now to change back, just think about how you see yourself in the mirror in the morning. Think about your room, your friends. Think about everything you're familiar with and imagine yourself there."

My brother, the bear, closed his eyes. He sat like that for several moments and the air shimmered around him. The bear was gone and in its place was my brother. He stood up and tested his previously broken ankle.

He turned to Mom and grinned. "When can I do that again?"

My alarm went off and I slapped it quiet. I didn't have to fake a headache to convince Mom I should stay home from school. I was so thankful for her medivoyance. I didn't

Shifting Dreams

want to hang out in bed all day like she thought I should, but I knew I couldn't deal with the teachers droning on and on about whatever it is they think is important. Besides, it was a nice day and I wanted to check on something.

Everyone left for school and work. Then I got myself ready and walked to the forest on the edge of town. Vin told us we shouldn't be there, but I had this feeling I couldn't shake.

I found the clearing, sat down, and waited. I closed my eyes to relax and hopefully get rid of my headache. I must have fallen asleep because when I opened my eyes, it was hot and the sun was shining directly over me.

Apparently, it was all a waste of time. I stood up and brushed the pine needles off my pants. I walked back to the path, watching the ground for giant roots. I knew those suckers were just waiting to trip the unsuspecting and the clumsy. I'd just jumped over one particularly mangy-looking shrub when I noticed there was someone standing on the path.

At first, all I saw were his shoes – big, black zombie-stomping boots. His long legs were covered in dark jeans, which covered a butt that was to-die-for. He wasn't big and built, but his arms gave me the idea that he worked out in some way. His hair was blond and scruffy and long, just like I liked it.

I must have made some noise just then, because he turned around to see me. I caught the square jaw and yummy lips before I looked up and saw his eyes. They were ringed with emerald and the bright green starburst was flecked with gold.

I knew those eyes. This was my wolf.

I suddenly didn't know what I was doing there. What if Vin was right and this guy hurt me for coming back into his territory?

I took a step back and he smiled. *Ohmygosh. He's going to kill me and he was going to enjoy it. What was I thinking?*

"Hey, I remember you." He took a step

toward me.

Could he smell my fear? Oh, I hoped he couldn't. I could only stand there and hope he had some other trait. Maybe he could talk to bugs or....oh, why did I have to come here today?

"Are you okay?"

He reached a hand toward me and I fell back. He wasn't going to get me without a fight. I scrambled around on the ground behind me and found a broken branch. I put my hand on it in case he came closer.

"I'm not going to hurt you!" He stepped back onto the path and I felt stupid. And wet. My pants were covered in thick mud where I'd fallen.

I laughed nervously. I sure knew how to make a first impression. I still wasn't sure what was going on, but it seemed like he wasn't going to hurt me. He stood still while I stood up and tried to brush off as much of the mud as possible.

"I'm sorry. I guess you scared me is all." I examined him more closely. Man, those eyes were amazing. "My friend told me that…well, that doesn't matter."

"Your friend told you that wolves like to eat little girls for dinner and use their bones as toothpicks," he said with a big grin. "I get it."

When he said it like that, it sounded even worse. I blushed and glanced around. I felt like an idiot.

He smiled. "I'm Leo."

"Hi, Leo. I'm Tessa," I said. "I feel stupid. I came out here looking for…well, and then I was scared when you…." I groaned. This was not turning out anything like I had imagined.

Leo grinned again. "Not a problem. Were you just leaving, or would you like to sit with me for a while?" He pointed back at the clearing where I'd fallen asleep earlier.

Shifting Dreams

"Yeah, I can stay for a bit." I turned around and walked back to the clearing.

We sat and stared at each other. I laughed nervously and brushed my hair behind my ear. I didn't know how to start. It's not like we were in the same classes and we could talk about the homework assignments or anything.

Thankfully, he knew what to say. "So, Tessa, you live around here, I take it?"

"Yeah, I live in Shadow Hills. You?"

"I live close. There's a group of cabins nearby. I live with my uncle and a few of his friends."

This whole time we were making eye contact. I couldn't stop staring. His eyes were just so…remarkable. I was having a hard time seeing him as a terrifying wolf, but I knew that's what he was.

I finally caught what he was saying. "Your uncle?"

"Yeah. Uncle Dev. He took me in after my parents died." He paused.

I didn't know what was up, but I figured it would be impolite to ask. "Oh. Is he cool?"

"Yeah." He nodded. "Enough about me, though. What about you? What's your family like?"

"My parents are cool…usually. I have an older brother, Tony. He's mostly a jerk, but he has his decent moments."

"Is that who you were out here with yesterday? Your brother?" Leo's nostrils flared, and his eyes flashed. I mean, literally flashed – they got brighter and then went back to normal. *Ha. Like anything around here is even close to being normal.*

"No, that was my friend Vin. And Chloe. We were doing a homework assignment." I could swear he growled when I said Vin's name. *Okay, this was totally weird.* I stood up. "I should probably go. I need to be home in case my parents decide to check up on me."

Leo stood and walked with me to the path. I felt his hand on my arm and shivered at the jolt I felt. Static electricity – it's gotta be.

"Maybe I'll see you again, Tessa." He smiled, and he was back to his dreamy self.

"I'd like that." I smiled. I knew my parents would probably flip, but whatever. They didn't control my life.

I walked home and went to my room. I lay on my bed and smiled at the stars on my ceiling. That boy was yummy. I was still thinking of him when I fell asleep.

We were sitting at the table, eating dinner. Mom made fried chicken and peas. Dad was raving about them when the doorbell rang. He went to answer it.

"Mallory? What are you doing here? You weren't supposed to be here until tomorrow night!" I heard Dad say.

Aunt Mallory was here early! I stood up and rushed to the door. I threw my arms around my favorite aunt. She traveled around the world a lot, so we didn't get to see her often. But she always brought gifts from foreign places. My favorite has always been the painting she bought from a street vendor in Paris. It was the Eifel Tower in purples and blues. It was the reason I wanted to be an artist in Paris.

"Hello, my beautiful Contessa!" Mallory gave me the nickname Contessa when I was five. She'd just come back from Italy and decided it fit me. "You have grown so much. You look so much like your mom when she was your age."

She pulled her bag through the door behind her and handed it to me. "Be a dear and take my luggage to my room. And check the front pocket. I think I left something in there." She grinned, and I knew where to look for my present.

I dragged her bag to the guest room and plopped it on the bed. I unzipped the front pocket and pulled out a beautiful gold necklace. It was one of those circle necklaces, a non-choking choker. Hanging from the ring was a yellow cat's eye pendant hanging from a swirling gold setting.

I ran out to the living room and hugged Aunt Mallory again. "Thank you, thank you, thank you! This is beautiful! Where did you get it?" I was so excited.

"I found it in a little shop in Hawai'i. It reminded me of you."

I woke up to my stomach rumbling. The smell of food dragged me downstairs to the kitchen, where Mom was making fried chicken. I paused and thought about my dream. I shook my head. It had to be a coincidence. I helped Mom set the table when Dad got home. Then we all sat and Mom brought out the food.

"Honey, this chicken is fantastic as always. I'm pretty sure I could eat this every-" Dad was cut off by the doorbell.

I knew who it was before Dad even opened the door. "Aunt Mallory," I breathed.

"Mallory! What are you doing here? You weren't supposed to get here until tomorrow night!"

I walked out to the living room and hugged my aunt. This was just weird. I grabbed her bag and walked back to the guest room.

"Contessa, my love, don't forget to look in the front zippered pocket!" Mallory yelled.

I pulled out the necklace. It was just as I'd pictured it in my dream, down to the last golden swirl. I stared at it. That was no dream. Aunt Mallory's arrival meant that I had seen the future. *Ohmygosh! This has happened before!*

I ran out of the room, still clutching the necklace. I ran upstairs to my room and searched through my backpack. I found my notebook and flipped through pages. There it was. The sketch I had made the first day in algebra. The profile of a boy with a square jaw and beautiful eyes. A wolf's eyes. Leo's eyes.

How could I have drawn such an accurate picture of him when I had never even met him? How did I know Aunt Mallory was going to be early? And what about the necklace? What was going on with me?

"Tessa, honey! Are you going to come finish dinner with us?" Dad yelled from the living room.

"Coming!" I had to figure this out. I had to know that I wasn't going insane. I couldn't tell my parents what was going on until I knew what it was. I had to act normal.

I put the necklace on and ran downstairs. I hugged Aunt Mallory and thanked her for the necklace. It was beautiful. When she went on about her most recent travels, I didn't pay much attention. It felt like all of my blood was rushing to my head. I could feel it pounding through my veins. So when I claimed a headache after dinner, it wasn't a lie.

I went to my room and sat at my desk. I wrote down all of my recent dreams. The necklace. The football game. The cave. The last hadn't happened yet, but I figured it was just a matter of time.

I picked up the book from school. *Shifters: A History.* Turning to the page about traits and ability levels, I scoured for more information. There wasn't much. It seemed like the book was written for us to learn the basics so we were barely prepared for whenever we learned more in class later.

Or maybe they didn't write about it because our parents were supposed to teach us everything. I didn't want to ask my mom any more questions. And Dad was a bust when it came to helping me study. He always sent me to Mom. It wasn't that he wasn't smart or anything, he just hated schoolwork. Not that I could blame him.

My head hurt, and I noticed it was almost midnight. Despite the fact that I'd had two naps that day, I had to get some sleep. Maybe tomorrow I would be able to figure something out.

I tossed and turned all night and didn't dream, which was excellent. I didn't think I could deal with any more weirdness.

When I woke up in the morning, I had bags under my eyes and my skin was blah. I shrugged and put extra makeup on and hoped nobody would notice. Somebody did.

"What happened to you?" Chloe asked when I met her at the corner. "You look like death."

"Thanks, great to see you too."

"You know what I mean. Are you sick or something?"

"Or something. Chloe, I-" I stopped. I didn't know what to say, so I shrugged instead

Chloe stared at me strangely. "What's up? Talk to me, T."

"You'll think I'm crazy." She'd never believe this, not without proof. But what proof did I have?

"Of course, you're crazy." She threw her arm over my shoulder, which was tough since she was several inches shorter than me. "You have to be to be friends with me!"

I gave her a half-hearted smile. "Yeah, you're right." I took a deep breath and let it all out in one big rush of words. "I keep having these dreams and I think I'm getting some kind of psychic ability and I'm freaked out and I don't think I can talk to anyone about it."

Chloe stopped walking and stared at me, her face blank. "Well, that's sweet. Did your invisible friend tell you that?"

"Hey, girls, how's it going?" Vin joined us when we reached the school.

"Tessa thinks she's psychic. What number am I thinking of?" Chloe closed her eyes and scrunched her entire face in concentration.

I rolled my eyes. "Like that's hard. Thirteen." I smacked her shoulder. "Come on, I'm serious!"

"It was thirteen! Oh, sweet and sour sauce! My best friend is psychic!" Chloe pretended to swoon into Vin's arms, and giggled.

Vin lifted Chloe to her feet. "It is hard to believe, Tessa. Do you have any proof?"

There it was again, where was my proof? I sighed. Then I remembered I did have proof. "Tony is going to be a bear on his birthday. Come over Saturday morning and you'll see."

Chapter Five

I somehow got through the rest of the week without any crazy dreams. I woke up Saturday feeling excited and nervous at the same time. I was excited because I would prove to my friends that I wasn't crazy. But then, if I wasn't crazy, I had no idea what I was going to do.

Chloe showed up early. We've been friends forever, so she knew the birthday routine. My parents made a breakfast feast. Eggs, bacon, waffles – you name it, we had it on the table.

Tony's best friend, Mark, walked in, followed by Vin. Mark has been Tony's best friend since forever. He was a running back on the football team. Not much taller than me, most people wonder why he didn't get immediately squished. But then they see him play. He has great reflexes. He's not the fastest player on the field, but there wasn't much he could do about that, I guess. I'd found out this week that his other form is a box turtle.

"Morning, Mr. Brooks," Mark said.

Dad nodded in response and handed him a plate. "Dig in, boys." he said as he turned back to the stove, where the last batch of bacon was sizzling in a pan.

"Sit down and eat before Tony gets here." Chloe told Vin. "Seriously. Try the fluffy egg stuff over there. Mr. Brooks makes the best Dutch babies." She threw a couple of pancakes on her plate before finding a spot to sit.

"What are Dutch babies?" Vin stared at them skeptically.

"German pancakes. Here, eat it with lemon juice and powdered sugar." I handed him a plate full of food and loaded up my own.

Vin sat and put a small bite in his

mouth. His eyes got big and he shoveled more in his mouth.

I grinned. I'd created a monster. I grabbed some before he went back for seconds.

Tony limped in on his crutches and saw everyone eating. "Hey! Whose birthday is it? I should be allowed to eat first!" Tony grumbled and shoveled food on a plate until stuff started falling off.

"Happy birthday, Tony," I said around the food in my mouth. If he had his way, he'd eat first and second and third…birthday or not.

We ate, and Tony and Mark discussed the game. Mark was glad that Tony would be back on the field for next week's game. They were playing against the Shadow Hills Rams rivals, the Beaumont Buccaneers. They definitely needed all the good players they had on the field.

We finished up and went out to the back yard. A bunch of adults made a lot of noise coming through the side fence. I recognized Chloe's parents, and then I saw the two adults I had seen in my dream. "Vin, your parents are here."

Vin glanced over, then back at me. "How did you know those are my parents?"

I shrugged and smiled. "Would you like to introduce us?"

We walked over and they introduced themselves. Chloe went to get her parents so they could all meet.

A moment later, there was a noise behind me. Tony sat in the middle of the yard, a pained look on his face. His eyebrows were scrunched together, his cheeks turning red. He shimmered and I knew what was coming next. All of the adults quickly changed into animals. Chloe's parents were both brown bears. Vin's parents turned into a ferret and a German Shepherd. Other adults were a deer, a large housecat, and a fox. I realized the fox was my aunt Mallory. *Sweet.*

Mom was the only one still in human form. She was talking softly to Tony, trying to keep him calm. "Don't fight it, Tony. Just let go."

Finally, Tony gave up and shimmered into…a bear. I caught Vin and Chloe's gazes. They both had huge, wide eyes and Chloe's mouth gaped open. Now they would believe me.

Mom murmured to my brother and he changed back. "When can I do that again?" Tony's grin was contagious.

Everyone else changed back and laughed. The adults resumed talking. Chloe, Vin and I went upstairs to my room. "Told you so."

"What the heck, Tessa!" Chloe was practically screaming. "How did you know?"

"I told you, I had a dream about it." I turned to Vin. "Do you know what it means? Do you have any idea what's going on?"

Vin stared at me for a couple of minutes. "It means that you're special," Vin finally said. "Tessa, we're not supposed to have any kind of ability until after we shift."

"So I really am a freak among freaks," I said. I didn't feel so weird about it now that it was out in the open, but I still had to adjust to it.

"Tessa, you have to tell your parents," Vin said, biting his lip. "This is serious. What if there's a reason nobody gets any abilities until after the first shift? What if it hurts you or something?"

"How could it hurt me?" I retorted. Then I remembered the headaches I'd been having. "Okay. I guess it can't hurt anymore than it already has."

I crossed the room to my sketch pad and showed them the picture I'd drawn of Leo. "I drew this on the first day of school. I didn't know who it was, and then I met him. It's one of the wolf shifters we met in the woods."

We all stared at it for a minute. Leo's face was there, just as I remembered it. His eyes were as amazing as I remembered them.

"Why did you draw a wolf shifter?" Vin looked puzzled. "Is this the only thing you drew?"

I thought about it. "Yeah, I guess so. I dreamt everything else." I glanced at the drawing again and frowned. Why was this the only image I'd drawn? Could I sit down and draw anything else? It definitely seemed likely. I may have to play around with it later.

We decided we couldn't do anything more until I talked to my parents, so we went back outside. The party had picked up a little. More of Tony's friends were there and they tossed the football to each other. Dad ran the grill and all the other dads hung around the fire. They were talking to each other intensely. They all kept glancing at Tony.

I saw all of the adults stiffen before I

heard the side gate open. I turned around as a man with dark hair and blue eyes walked into the yard. Another man walked behind him. He was much older, with a graying mustache and silver hair. I didn't pay attention to them because I could only stare at the person who walked in behind them. Leo.

They walked over to my dad and bowed their heads to him. He nodded back and held his hand out to Tony. Tony walked over and bowed his head at them. Dad and Tony acted like they were talking to the king or something.

"Devereaux, meet my son, Tony. Tony, this is Devereaux Munroe, his father, Russell, and his nephew, Leo," Dad was all stiff, his voice deeper than I'd ever heard.

"It is a pleasure to meet you," the man, Devereaux, said. "I hear you are in need of a large area to run, due to the size of your animal affinity. I am here to invite you to use my territory in the woods for this purpose. I only ask that you please limit your time there, and do not cross the fence into our personal space."

Dad bowed his head. Tony must have figured out this was a big deal because he bowed his head, too. "Thank you for your invitation. I appreciate your offer. I will follow your rules."

The man turned to leave. His nostrils flared and he turned to me. He glared back at Leo. There must have been some type of communication, because the man turned back to me, glowering.

He walked over and I had trouble breathing. I could practically feel the power, like a cloud surrounding this guy. His nostrils flared again and he took a deep breath. "You know Leo." It wasn't a question.

"Yes, sir. How-"

"I can smell him on you," he said. He glared at me. It felt like a warning. When he walked away, the old man and Leo followed him. Leo held my gaze until he looked down. I felt like he was ashamed of me.

Shifting Dreams

As soon as the gate shut behind them, someone grabbed my arm and dragged me inside the house. Dad turned me around abruptly. "What the hell was that about, Tessa?" Dad's eyes were wide. I could swear he was scared. He never cursed. "Where did you meet Leo, and why didn't you tell us about it?"

"I-I met Leo the other day and-"

"Why didn't you tell me you met a wolf?" Dad's face flushed. His eyes bulged. "What were you thinking? Do you even know what you did?"

I had never seen my dad like this. He never yelled. Especially in front of guests, who were all standing close to the back door that Dad hadn't closed behind us, listening.

"Go to your room! We'll talk about this later!" Dad stomped off.

I went to my room. I didn't know why Dad was so upset, but I would bet it had something to do with the fact that wolves were

JM Kline

considered dangerous.

I listened at the open bedroom window as Mom apologized to everyone. I saw people walk from the back yard to the front of the house and leave. Chloe glanced at my window with pity. She gave me a little wave and left with her parents. Vin mouthed, 'I'm sorry' before getting into the car with his parents.

I waited for my parents to come up and talk to me about what happened. It got dark a few hours later and they still hadn't come in. I was starting to get nervous when the door finally opened. I was surprised when I saw it wasn't either of my parents. It was my Aunt Mallory.

She had a plate of food in her hand, and my empty stomach reminded me that I'd missed dinner. I was hungry, but I stared at it for a second without reaching for it.

Aunt Mallory laughed. "It's not poisoned. Eat up."

I took a bite of spaghetti and my

stomach grumbled. I shoveled food in my mouth.

I barely paused when Aunt Mallory spoke. "Your parents are upset about what happened earlier," she started. "Frankly, I can't blame them. Wolf shifters are...unpredictable, at best. Having one know your scent is not a good thing – especially when that one is the alpha in the pack."

"Aunt Mallory, I don't even know what's going on. What was that all about, and why am I the one who is in trouble? Tony's the one they came for, right?" I'd, at least, understood that much of the situation.

My aunt sighed. "Yes, they came because of Tony. I guess you need some background on all of this. Okay." She took a deep breath, gathering her thoughts. "Wolf shifters were here first. They claimed this territory when it was still the Colorado Territory, quite some time ago. When other shifters tried to move here, there was some tension. Fights broke out. There was a lot of resentment.

"Eventually, the two groups came to an agreement. The wolf shifters would keep their rights on the 'hidden' territory, mainly the forest area. The rest of us would be allowed to build a town, Shadow Hills, and stay out of their way. The only exceptions to this would be the larger animal shifters. Those who would cause a panic among outsiders if they were in their animal forms in town are allowed to use the forest for running.

"We need to run in our other form on a regular basis, or we start to wither. Tony's shift into a bear meant that he needed the privacy of the forest. The alpha of the wolf shifters, Devereaux, came to give him access to their territory." She paused here.

I swallowed a half-chewed bite of noodles. "What about me? What did I do wrong?"

She frowned. "Tessa, when he turned to

you, we were all nervous. Nobody knew if we would have to fight to keep you safe. Like I said, they're unpredictable." She put her hand on my leg. "I am so glad nothing happened, but it was an unacceptable situation. I was terrified for you, Tessa."

Tears rolled down her face and I comprehended the danger. Aunt Mallory was never scared – even when she was kidnapped by a bunch of guys with guns in Mexico. "I promise I'll stay away, Aunt Mallory." I put my plate on my bed and leaned over to hug her.

When she stopped crying, I pulled back. Now that we had that figured out, I had to talk to her about the other thing. I looked down at my hands, squeezing my fingertips together nervously. "Can I ask you a question? You have to promise not to think I'm crazy."

She watched me carefully. "Okay. I promise."

"Have you ever heard of a shape shifter

who…can see the future?"

Aunt Mallory eyes widened with surprise. She leaned back and sat very still. "Tessa, are you trying to tell me something?"

"Yes." I took a deep breath. "I've been having dreams about the future. Vin told me that it was a big deal, so-"

Aunt Mallory grew pale. I thought she might faint away dead right there. Instead, she stood up and grabbed my arm and dragged me to the door. "Tessa, we have to tell your parents right now. We need to gather everyone we can and head into the mountains tonight. That boy is the least of your problems."

The terror in her voice was scaring me. "Wait a minute! What's wrong? What are you saying?"

She didn't stop, but pulled me even harder to the stairs. "If we don't force your change early, you're going to die."

Chapter Six

Aunt Mallory tore down the stairs, crushing my hand all the way. I had to hold on to the rail to keep from falling.

"Eva! Anthony!" she yelled to my parents. "We have bigger problems to deal with than wolves!"

Mom and Dad were sitting in the living room. They both stood up when we came in. "What's going on?" Mom asked.

"Eva, she's a clairvoyant. We need to gather everyone we can and head to the cave. We need to start the Ritual of Change. Now!"

I didn't understand anything she said, but my parents apparently did. They both got the same panicked look that my aunt had, and ran to their phones.

They spent the next twenty minutes calling pretty much everyone in town. I sat there and watched, getting more scared by the second. When they weren't paying attention, I sent a text to Chloe and told her to come over. I didn't care if I got in trouble for it, I needed my best friend.

The front door slammed open and Chloe rushed through it, almost knocking me over with a hug. Her parents walked into the house after her. "Tessa, my parents are totally spazzing out about you. What happened? What's going on?"

"I don't know," I said. "I told Aunt Mallory about the dreams and everyone started running around. They're calling everyone they know and nobody has told me anything."

Mom came over and put her hands on our shoulders. "Come into the kitchen, girls. Chloe, your parents are calling everyone I missed."

She brought us into the kitchen and sat

Shifting Dreams

us at the table. I could tell she was nervous and scared. Tears fell down her face.

"Mom, what is going on?"

"Tessa, nobody in the country has seen a clairvoyant in almost a century, and now my baby girl is one," she sobbed. "I can't believe I didn't see the signs. Now that I'm looking," she paused and scanned me from head to toe and sobbed. "I see it all!"

"Mom, it's not that big a deal. I have dreams. Dreams aren't going to kill me."

She sobbed even harder. Guess that was the wrong thing to say. "Tessa, you have a long road ahead of you, but first we need to force your change early." Mom wiped her eyes and took a couple of deep breaths. "You need to prepare yourself for the pain. It's going to hurt a lot more than a natural change, but it's better than the alternative."

This was not what I planned. A little pain on my seventeenth birthday, I was starting to come to terms with – if Mom was stressing this much about it, it was going to hurt. A lot.

"Can Chloe be there with me?" I would need a friend if I was going to get through this.

"No, honey," Mom said. She had finally calmed down and was taking deep breaths. "We don't know what form you'll take and we can't risk her safety."

"Can I at least have Tony? He can protect himself!" I couldn't breathe. I was in full-on panic mode at this point.

"Yes, we definitely need Tony there. His energy is so new and young that it will help you-" she paused.

I heard the unspoken *'help you with the massive amounts of pain you have to go through.'*

Dad came in. "We're ready." He came up to me and hugged me tightly. "It's going to be okay, sweetheart. You know we are all going to be there for you."

Shifting Dreams

Chloe's dad came in with a paper shopping bag. He pulled out what looked like a cloth potato sack.

"Tessa, you need to put this dress on." Dad grabbed it and handed it to me. I unfolded it and saw that it was made of white linen and only vaguely resembled a dress.

"I am not wearing this. It's disgusting!" I made a face and turned it around. It wasn't any better than the other side, and I couldn't decide which was supposed to go in the front. I crumpled it into a ball and threw it back in the bag.

Mom sighed. "It's not going to win you any fashion awards, but you can't wear your regular clothes. You can only shift into your other form if you're wearing all natural fibers. The ritual works best without barriers. We couldn't find anything else in your size on such short notice. It's either this or you go naked."

I blushed and pulled the dress back out.

Maybe it wasn't so bad after all. Chloe followed me up to my room so I could change.

It had only been a couple of weeks since I found out I was a shifter. I remembered the pact Chloe and I had made. Nothing would change between us. I snorted. Everything was changing. I needed something normal. I turned to Chloe.

"Stay here tonight. We can hang out and watch movies and eat ice cream when I get back," I told her. I couldn't let myself think about not coming back.

"Definitely. I'll run home while you're-" Chloe paused and closed her mouth. She narrowed her eyes and gave me a grin that was obviously for my benefit. "I'll be here with movies and junk food."

I didn't know what I'd do without her. I didn't know what to say, so I hugged her and we went downstairs, where our parents were all waiting.

Shifting Dreams

"Are you ready, sweetheart?" Mom put her hand on my arm.

"Ready as I'll ever be." I was so nervous, my hands shook.

We walked out to the cars and I got in. Tony was already sitting in the back seat, and I moved closer to him. As big of a pest as he normally was, he was my big brother and he always had my back when it mattered. He wrapped his arm around me and I felt warm and safe.

The drive felt too short but we stopped about an hour outside of town. When Dad parked, I got out and almost fell. My legs were weak and wobbly. I guess I was more nervous than I thought.

Tony threw his arm around my shoulders and we followed my parents onto a path. They suddenly turned left off the path and we walked through the dark woods. The cave appeared in front of us and the adults walked inside after taking off their shoes and putting them in a large pile outside the entrance. Tony and I lingered for a second. I was so not ready for this.

I took a deep breath, kicked off my sandals, and walked in. The cave was big and dark. The cluster of quartz in the center gave off a blue glow. I remembered this from my dream.

The walls and floor were smooth, which was good since I wasn't wearing shoes. I smelled the pine of the trees outside mixed with some kind of wet animal. I wondered what sort of animals would come in here. I was sure there weren't many who could stand to be in here. The air felt like it was filled with static electricity. I could swear my hair was flying around my face and I was grateful none of my friends could see me like this.

Dad was talking to a group of men. When he saw me, he came over. "Now, Tessa, we are all going to change first and then-"

Shifting Dreams

"I know, Daddy. I had this dream already."

Dad's face crunched in pain and I knew he was worried. He hugged me close and tight. Everyone was nervous and it wasn't making me any less so.

He let go and shimmered into his animal form. Everyone else had done the same and they were all waiting around the cave.

The humming began and I knelt on the quartz in the center. It was cold and hard and I wished this would end. Mom and Dad leaned into me and Tony sat in front of me. His big paws were in front of the quartz pedestal. He leaned in. His tongue darted out and he kissed my forehead.

"Ew! Gross. Bear spit!" I reached my hand out and gave his front paw a scratch. I couldn't stay mad at him. I had to forgive him for being gross. This time.

The humming got louder and the

animals around me formed a sort of spiral shape. My aunt stood behind Tony and the biggest, strongest animals were close behind her. I recognized Mr. Rogers, the turtle, up against the wall. Apparently everyone in town was here. I was glad for the ugly linen dress.

Suddenly, I felt searing pain work its way slowly up from my toes. When it hit my hips, I bent forward in agony. My muscles twitched as it slowly worked up my back, and I couldn't help but scream when my neck popped and burned. My head exploded.

The pain stopped as soon as it started. I was curled up on the pedestal, crying, finally able to breathe when I heard my dad say it was over. I slowly opened my eyes and saw that the cave had gotten bigger. The bears surrounded me and Mom was flying above me. I looked down and saw paws.

They were big and black, with wicked-looking claws peeking out of the fur. I turned my head to see my body. It was long and covered in shiny black fur. Peering closer, I saw faint outlines of spots scattered around my new body. I felt a tickle and the fur-covered skin twitched in response. My long black tail was swishing back and forth.

"No. Freaking. Way," I said. At least, I tried to say it. All that came out was a weird groaning growl.

I stood up and stretched. My body felt so different, but it still felt like me. I rolled around on the floor and rubbed my face against the side of the quartz. This was amazing.

I stood up and glanced around. Everyone was still watching me and I figured they probably wanted to see me change back. I thought about Tony's birthday party and what Mom had said to him about changing.

I closed my eyes and thought about my room at home. My drawings covered the walls and the glowing stars scattered across the ceiling. I thought about standing in front of my mirror and remembered what I saw. I thought about my long, black hair and my light brown eyes. I imagined my pointed nose, and my long, slender fingers.

I felt a small jolt of electricity and opened my eyes. I looked down and saw my hands and the ugly dress and my too-big feet. Apparently, I was back.

Dad's arms wrapped around me. Mom pressed up against my other side and they both held me for a while.

When they finally let go, I could see everyone staring at me like they had never seen me before. The more they stared, the more self-conscious I felt. Like this whole situation wasn't hard enough already, now even the adults didn't know what to do with me.

I'd had enough.

I turned and walked out of the cave, slipped on my sandals, and headed back the way we came. Just because they think they saved my life, didn't mean everyone had permission to be so rude. Chloe was waiting for me at home and she was the only one I could think of who wouldn't treat me like I was different.

Hearing footsteps behind me, I knew that Tony had followed. Fine. It's not like I could drive home anyway. Hopefully Dad gave him the keys so I didn't have to sit around and wait. My adrenaline had worn off and I was definitely feeling the chill. We were high enough on the mountain that the air was always cold. I didn't want to freeze while I waited.

I got to the car and it unlocked. I pulled the door open and climbed into the passenger seat.

Tony got in and turned on the car. He sat there for a minute to let it warm up. I could tell he wanted to say something.

"What? Did I steal your thunder? So sorry I ruined your birthday." I knew I was being rude, but I didn't care.

"Tessa, that was amaze-pants!" Tony exclaimed, with one of his made-up words. "You are no longer just my kid sister. I don't have to pull my punches with you anymore. It is on!"

I glanced at him and saw the grin on his face. He was excited for me, but I knew my brother. He was more excited that he thought he could still kick my butt. I grinned back at him, thankful that some things never changed. "Better watch your back. You're not the biggest, baddest Brooks anymore."

Tony winked and drove us home. When we pulled into the driveway, the light in my room was on. *My best friend pulls through again.* I thanked Tony and jumped out of the car. I ran through the house and up to my room. I couldn't wait to get that ugly linen dress off.

Chloe sat at my desk and typed away on my laptop. She was in a chat program and I wondered who she was talking to. "Who is GreyMan443?"

She glanced back at me. "It's Vin. I was trying to see if he knew anything, but I ended up telling him everything your mom told us." Chloe smiled and rolled her eyes. "So much for him being an expert,"

When I was in my comfy cotton stretchy shorts and a matching tank top, I flopped onto my bed.

"So what are we watching tonight?" I looked around and saw the pile of chips, cookies, cookie dough, and ice cream. My stomach growled. I was starving. "Oh, let's go make some pizza rolls or something. I haven't eaten and I swear I could eat a horse."

I went downstairs and Chloe followed me. I threw the food in the microwave before I turned around to find her staring at me. She wasn't going to let me ignore what happened tonight. I sighed. "Okay, here's what happened. Weird ritual, mega pain, and I changed."

Chloe lifted her eyebrow. "That's it?

Wow, you must be something totally lame if you won't even tell me what you changed into."

I paused. I hadn't said the words yet. I almost felt like if I didn't say them, they wouldn't be real. I looked at Chloe and I knew she wasn't going to let it go.

I took a deep breath and blurted it out. "I'm a panther."

Chapter Seven

Chloe's eyes got wide. She burst into a smile.

"That is so freaking cool, Tessa!"

The microwave dinged and I took my time getting the pizza rolls out. I grabbed a paper towel. Then another.

I stared at the twining vines and pink flowers on the plate. If Mom knew I had used her nice dishes in the microwave, she would have kittens. I giggled to myself and thought about how she really did have a kitten...almost sixteen years ago.

I took a deep breath and held it. I did not want to face my best friend. She wanted to talk about what happened. I wanted nothing more than to erase the last few weeks of my life. Tonight changed everything forever. I didn't know how I was going to deal with any of it. I knew I would have to figure it all out eventually, but not now. I turned back to Chloe. "Chloe, I love you, but right now I want to forget tonight ever happened and pretend like we're normal for a while. Can we please go upstairs and eat until we're sick and watch movies until we pass out?"

Chloe's eyes narrowed for a second, and then her face cleared. "Let's go, T. I hope you made enough pizza rolls for me. I'm starving." She twined her arm in mine. "But you know I am going to force you to talk in the morning. There is no way something this cool is going to happen to my best friend and I'm going to leave it alone."

Of course she would expect answers but, for now, we could have a girly sleepover. No animals. No premonitions. Just two girls eating junk food and watching chick flicks.

Two hours and two pints of ice cream

later, we were watching movie number two, and I heard my parents walk in. They must have had a huge, long meeting after I left the cave. I'm sure they all had lots to say about me. I'm sure they planned out the rest of my life like I was some "Chosen One" or something.

Chloe and I glanced at each other. I made a face. I hoped they didn't want to talk about anything. I wanted one night before the craziness returned.

A knock on the door let me know that wasn't going to happen. I sighed and went to open it. My scream was cut short when I realized the bear standing in the hallway was my brother. And all those pointy, white teeth were supposed to be a grin.

"Go away, Tony. Shouldn't you be getting your beauty sleep or something? You need it."

Tony shimmered back to himself and grinned some more. "Just wanted to let you know what to expect from now on, Squirt. No place is safe from me!" He laughed maniacally as he walked to his room and closed the door.

"Ugh, that's exactly what I need," I said. Chloe was trying not to smile, but she sucked at it. "I see I'm not going to get any sympathy from you."

"Why would you? I'm so jealous! You don't have to wait the next two years to find out what the change feels like, or what you're going to be! Plus, you are a freaking panther!" She shook her head. "Nope, no sympathy here. Although…."

She narrowed her eyes. I could practically see thoughts running through her head.

"Although what? What are you thinking?"

"Well," she paused, "maybe you can use this new power of yours for good. Maybe…try to see what the future has in store for, say…me?" She raised an eyebrow, a glint in her eyes revealed her excitement.

"I don't know if it works that way, Chloe. Everything I've ever seen was kind of random."

"But you saw your brother's change. That's something, right?" Chloe looked at me with big puppy eyes.

"No way. You promised I had tonight before you would bug me about anything." I crossed my arms and glared at her.

"Ha! You should have made me pinkie swear." She pouted. "Fine, I'll let it go. But we are going to have fun with this."

Only Chloe would think that random visions of the future were fun. I shook my head. At least she wasn't weirded out by it all. I was so thankful I had such a great best friend.

We finished the movie and decided to go to sleep. It had been a long day.

***

I woke up the next day, and I was so happy that it was Sunday. I didn't have to even leave my room if I didn't want to. Well, in theory anyway.

Tony had obviously decided it is his new "brotherly duty" to get me to shift and fight him, to see who is stronger and faster. I wasn't looking forward to the surprises he would have in store for me.

I didn't want to change. Once was enough for me, for now. I knew I would eventually want to try it out and see what it was like. I remembered how much I liked it at the time, but I didn't want to actually go through it again. The last time hurt.

Sure, it was probably because they had to force my change, but I couldn't be sure. Tony wasn't in pain every time he did it, but he was seventeen. He was supposed to be able to shift. I wasn't.

True to her word, Chloe attacked as soon as we finished breakfast and went back to my room. "Okay, so let me see." Chloe stared at me expectantly, leaning against me like she could force the change.

"What? No! Get off!" I pushed her away. "I want to stay human, thank you very much."

"That's nice." Chloe poked my arm. "But you're not. So let me see. Or else I'm going to find your brother and tell him to get you while you're in the shower."

I stared at her. Her arms were crossed and she had a stubborn look on her face. She would totally do it. So much for best friends sticking together.

"Ugh. Fine," I gave in. "But I'll remember this and I will get you back some day."

Chloe shrugged. "Whatever. Now quit stalling."

I sighed and closed my eyes. I thought about the pictures I'd seen of panthers. I figured if I had to think about how I normally looked to shift into a human, I should think of panthers to look like that.

My body felt incredibly tight, like all of my muscles tensed up all at once. It was painful, but not nearly as bad as I'd feared.

I opened my eyes to find Chloe staring at me with awe. She examined my new cat's body, like she was trying to find a foot that I'd forgotten to change or something.

"Wow," she whispered. "You are so beautiful. Can I touch you?"

From anyone else, that question would have earned a swipe with my new, sharp talons. I grumbled and leaned forward. Again, I knew she wouldn't let it go. Might as well embrace the weirdness.

Her hand was gentle as she ran it back from my shoulder to rib cage. Then she ran it the other way. There was no way to describe that feeling except "wrong." It felt like a static shock to each individual strand of hair, and caused me to shiver.

I moved away and hissed. She got the message. But then she started poking me.

Thinking about my human form, I shifted back, about to give her a piece of my mind. How dare she poke me? But my rant was cut short due to my extreme lack of a shirt.

I stood in front of her for a few seconds before I knew what else had happened. I had my jeans on, but I had nothing covering my top. Absolutely. Nothing.

"Eep!" I quickly turned around and pulled a shirt out of my closet. "What the heck happened?"

Of course, Chloe couldn't answer because she was laughing too hard. Glad she got a kick out of it. I was so going to get revenge.

I glanced at my feet and saw a shredded

mass of purple fabric. That was my favorite shirt! "Mom!" I yelled.

I heard her walk down the hallway a few seconds before she opened my bedroom door.

"What is it?" Mom asked quietly. She looked tired.

I guess she stayed up way later than usual last night. I felt bad. "Sorry I woke you up."

"It's fine, sweetie. What's up?" She yawned.

"Why did my shirt fall apart?" I pointed to the pile of purple on my floor.

Mom stared at it blankly for a second before she seemed to snap out of it. "Oh, I'm so sorry, honey. I didn't even think about it." Mom stepped in the doorway and leaned against the wall. "You can't wear anything that isn't a natural fiber when you change. Your jeans are usually safe, because they're cotton. But you need to pay attention to the labels from now on."

Shifting Dreams

I pouted at what used to be a shirt and silently mourned my loss. So much for stretchy jeans – they had spandex. "Okay. Thanks, Mom." I sighed.

Mom smiled and shuffled out.

My shredded pile of ex-shirt made me sigh again. Just great. I glanced at my closet and had a terrible thought.

I grabbed a shirt at random. Cotton-spandex. Then another. Polyester-cotton. And another. And another. Eventually, I had a pile of clothes on the floor that I couldn't wear while shifting. The only thing I had left in my closet was a ratty old Mickey Mouse t-shirt and a white tank top that told everyone I had been to Martin's Crab House.

I threw myself onto my bed. "I have nothing to wear!" I whined to Chloe. "How could my parents let me buy all those clothes if I wasn't going to be able to wear them? What am I supposed to do?"

Chloe sat next to me with a grin on her face.

"This is not the time for you to be laughing at me! I practically have to go to school naked from now on!"

Chloe kept grinning and shook her head. "No, T. You get to go shopping. Come on. Let's get Tony to drive us to LaRuss. Your parents owe you a new wardrobe."

LaRuss was the big fashion outlet in Denver. Their prices were high, but they used all-natural fabrics in a totally humane way. I never tried to talk my parents into letting me shop there. I always figured they would say 'no' because of the cost. But where else could I go to get clothes I could wear?

"Yeah, I guess I can get away with that now, huh?" I smiled and kicked the pile of clothes. "Especially if I tell them I'm donating all of my old clothes to the shelter."

It didn't take long for me to talk my

parents into letting us go. But first, I had to say goodbye to Aunt Mallory. She was leaving for another great adventure, though I had no idea what she could find interesting or exciting about the frozen expanse of northern Canada.

I hugged her as she left. "I'm going to miss you like crazy, Aunt Mallory."

"Oh, me too, Contessa." She touched the necklace I wore around my neck. "It really does suit you. More than I could've guessed. I hope you like it."

"I love it. It'll make me think of you." I hugged her again. "Be safe, okay? Don't let those Canadian rabbits cause you too much trouble."

"Don't worry about me. I'm foxy." Her eyes glinted in amusement, a small smile playing on her mouth.

I rolled my eyes. "Ha-ha. You're so funny."

And then she was gone. Dad drove

down the street, bringing his sister-in-law to the airport, where new adventures awaited. I sighed and worked on convincing Tony to bring Chloe and me into town to shop. Finally, I promised a backyard brawl. He practically ran to his car. Too bad for him, I didn't say *when* I would fight him. Guess he should have asked.

He must have felt good about himself, because he let Chloe and I listen to our music, instead of his normal classic rock station. We dropped my old clothes at the donation spot, picked up Mark, and headed into Denver.

When we got to LaRuss, I instantly fell in love with the place. It was a huge warehouse-like building, full of racks of clothes.

Tony and Mark disappeared to the guys' side. We were supposed to send a text when we were ready to go.

I was in the middle of browsing a rack of t-shirts when I felt someone watching me. I looked around and saw him.

Leo wore a tight black shirt and his normal gigantic leather boots. His jeans showed off his muscular legs. He looked so good. I wondered how he'd found me, but I didn't have to wonder for long.

"Hey, Tessa," he said with an amazingly sexy smile. "I knew it the second you walked in."

"How?" Was he stalking me?

"I could, uhm," he was obviously embarrassed, "smell you. But you do smell a little different now."

He came closer. He was only six inches away from me now, and he closed his eyes and took a deep breath. His eyes suddenly opened, and I was again shocked at how gorgeous they were. They flashed.

"You smell wild, like deep forest." He came closer. I could feel his breath on my temple. I closed my eyes and shivered. "You smell like the hunt."

I felt him pull away. It made me open my eyes. His gaze intent, he stared at me. "What is going on? You shouldn't smell this different. You are too young to-" he studied my face. "When did this happen? How?"

"I uh-" How could I explain what happened? Would I get in trouble for telling him? Why didn't my parents tell the wolf-shifters what happened? Wasn't I supposed to get that same "privilege to run" that Tony got?

I was rescued from making an ass of myself when Chloe came over with a stack of clothes. "Tessa, I found some great deals over-" she stopped when she saw Leo.

"Leo, this is my best friend Chloe. Chloe, this is Leo." I hoped she wouldn't embarrass herself by running, like I had the first time I'd met him.

"Oh." she took a step back. "Hi, Leo. Nice to meet you."

I'm sure he could tell that she wasn't

excited to meet him. She was not very subtle when she backed away and hid behind a clothes rack.

Leo got the point. "I'll let you get back to shopping." He turned to me and leaned in close. I could smell the peppermint on his breath and feel his warm breath on my neck. "You will tell me what is going on. Soon."

Chapter Eight

I watched Leo walk away and shivered. I felt warmth in my stomach that instantly went away when Chloe smacked my arm.

"What was that about? Are you crazy? Do you know how much trouble you could get in if your dad found out you were talking to him?"

I thought she was going to hyperventilate or something. "I didn't even know he was here until he talked to me. Come on, I need new clothes. Oh, what is that?" I ignored her frown to search through the pile of clothes she'd brought me.

She'd found some great stuff, and I was actually distracted by the clothes, instead of just pretending so she would get off my back. I tried

Shifting Dreams

on everything and got rid of half of it. I moved along the racks and looked at clothes. I picked out a v-neck purple hoodie and wondered what Leo would think of it.

I shook my head. I didn't know what I would do about him. It's not like my parents would ever let me date him. I didn't know him that well, either. So why couldn't I stop thinking about him?

I'm sure my mom would tell me it was hormones. But I swear there's something different about him. I felt like I had to get to know him. I wondered if he had the same feelings.

After spending almost twice as much money as my dad told me I could – which was still less than what Mom told me I could spend – we met up with my brother and Mark and had lunch. Then we took Chloe home.

I couldn't wait to get some of my new clothes on. As soon as I unloaded the car, I ran to my room, changed, and admired my new look. The cat's eye necklace Aunt Mallory had given me seemed to complete the outfit. My wardrobe was picked with that in mind. It was all more elegant, more grown up.

I tried to convince myself that I hadn't bought most of it with Leo in mind but, staring at the flirty, lacy bottom of my new purple top, I knew better. It's not like he'd notice, being a guy. Regardless, it made me feel good to change up my style once in a while.

With a sigh, I hung up the rest of my clothes. School was going to suck. It wasn't so bad last week when I was the normal kind of weirdo. But now, I was the only one in the class who had changed, and I didn't know what to do about it.

I was sure most people would be like Chloe and want to see me change. But I didn't want to be a sideshow attraction. It was fine for my best friend, but everyone else? I would have to prepare to tell them all "no." That would earn

Shifting Dreams

me popularity points. Not!

And what about the other thing? I was focused on the shifting – I could at least partially deal with that part. I had no idea how I would deal with the fact that I could see the future. I thought about Chloe last night, asking me to see into her future. That may have been the first request, but it wouldn't be the last.

No, I didn't want to deal with that right now, or ever.

I went downstairs to the kitchen to see if Mom wanted help with dinner. She wasn't there. I heard Tony's music blaring from his room, but it looked like we were the only ones home. Weird. Nothing ever happened on Sundays.

I decided to make the most of my afternoon and do what I did best. Draw.

I went to my room and pulled open my desk drawer. It was empty. Well, okay. Not empty, but underneath the ruler, calculator, all the various erasers, there was nothing. No pencils. No pens. No paper.

I thought maybe I'd moved it all to my bag, so I checked there. There was trash and a few school books, but otherwise – nothing. Panic tightened my chest. What had happened to my things?

I searched under my bed, in my closet, anywhere I could think that I would leave them. Nothing. None of my old artwork was in my room, and I couldn't find any paper to draw on.

Then, it dawned on me. How could I be so stupid? My parents went through my stuff when I was out and took all of my drawing supplies. But, why?

I stopped cold. They'd seen my picture of Leo, and now they had it.

I grabbed my phone and pounded the screen to call Mom's cell phone. It rang and rang and rang. Of course, she wasn't going to pick up the phone. She felt guilty. She'd better feel guilty! She stole my things!

I tried Dad's number next. Same thing. I stomped to Tony's room and threw open the door without knocking.

"What do you know about this?" I yelled. I was furious. How dare they get into my personal belongings?

Tony and Mark were playing a video game. Tony paused it before responding. "What do you mean? What am I supposed to know?" He had a stupid look on his face. He wasn't much of an actor, so I figured he didn't know anything.

"Mom and Dad stole all of my drawings and all of my paper and pencils! Did you know this was going to happen?" I was slowly getting less angry with him. He was obviously a big, dumb idiot. Though if he was an idiot for not knowing anything, what did that make me?

"They did? Why would they do that?" He glanced at Mark, who shrugged.

I sighed. Might as well tell them. It's not

like it could hurt anything anymore than it already did. "I drew a picture of Leo – that wolf-shifter – before I met him. I don't know how they found out about it, but suddenly my stuff is gone and that's the only thing that I can think of."

Tony's big bushy eyebrows rose about a quarter of an inch in surprise. He wasn't one for expressions. "You drew a picture of someone you didn't know? That's cool, Tessa. I wonder if that's part of your new poooweeerrrsss." He said the last bit in his stupid spooky voice and wiggled his fingers and hands at me.

"Ha-ha, you're a big help. Thanks for nothing," I said. I walked out and slammed the door behind me. I heard them laughing, and loud music let me know that the game had resumed.

I stood in the hallway and thought about where my parents could be. Maybe Tony was on to something. Maybe drawing was connected to my power to see the future in some way. Crazier things had happened. Like me being able to see the future.

I went back in Tony's room and searched for paper, ignoring his protests when I walked in front of the TV. Nothing. They must have taken away all the paper in the house. Either that, or Tony didn't know the meaning of homework. It wouldn't surprise me.

I grabbed my new shoes and purple hoodie before leaving the house. Anywhere was better than the House of Suffocated Dreams.

I wandered around for a bit before I saw that I was close to the edge of the forest, and the clearing where I'd first met Leo. I headed in that direction.

When I found the clearing, I sat. I breathed deeply to clear my head, and I heard a noise. I turned to see Leo in all his delicious glory.

"You always seem to know where to find me," I said. To be honest, I was hoping he would. He seemed to be the only one who didn't have new expectations for me.

"Yes, I do," he said quietly. He sat across from me and stared. It should have been uncomfortable, but I actually didn't mind at all. "I need to know what's happened with you, Tessa Brooks. You're…different. I don't understand what I'm sensing from you."

"Sensing?" I had a small hope that he meant he had some psychic, otherworldly ability too.

"Yes, you smell different. You sound different. You look different. And it's completely impossible, because you're not seventeen yet."

I sighed. Right. Those senses.

"You don't know the half of it," I said. I didn't know what to tell him. I didn't know what my parents would want me to...wait. Why did I care what my parents wanted? They obviously didn't care enough about my feelings to talk to me before stealing my things.

Shifting Dreams

I didn't know how to tell Leo about everything that had happened since I last saw him. The best way to tell him was to show him. Standing, I thought about my other form. Black, a long, swishing tail, yellow eyes.

I had to give him credit. He barely blinked when I changed. He studied my form. "How is this possible?"

I changed back and hoped my new clothes would still be there. I glanced down. Good, still dressed. And my necklace hadn't fallen off or anything. *I'd have to ask someone about that later*, I thought, sitting back down. "Where should I even start?" So many things had happened over the last couple weeks, I didn't even know where the weirdness began.

"Start where you can shift and you're not seventeen yet. I mean, you're not, right? Because you sure don't seem like you're old enough." His gaze swept over me.

I felt all tingly wherever his eyes went. I

fought a shiver. "No, I'm not seventeen. I'll be sixteen next month. I went through this ritual in a cave in the mountains. I was forced to change early," I told him.

Leo's face changed when I mentioned the cave. "I think I know the cave. But who forced you to change, and why?" he asked me with an attitude.

I wondered if he thought it was some big conspiracy or something. "They made me change so I wouldn't die, okay? That's it. There's nothing else to say about it," I said. No way was I going to tell him the rest if he was going to act like that.

"Wait, why would you die? What aren't you saying?" He leaned toward me.

"Nothing. Forget about it." I stood up, angry. I wasn't about to put up with some over-controlling guy.

"Tessa, I'm sorry." He held out a hand. "Please, sit. I'm confused is all. I won't push anymore. I promise."

I considered him, trying to figure out if he was telling the truth. "Fine. Look," I paused. "I don't want to get into everything right now. It's a lot of stuff to deal with, and I don't know that much about you."

"Then let's get to know each other." Leo smiled and gestured to the ground in front of him.

He appeared so apologetic, I couldn't resist. Smiling, I took his hand and sat. My hand tingled where we touched. I couldn't control the goosebumps that showed up on my arms. When he dropped my hand, it felt cold and empty. I probably shouldn't care so much about something like that, but it had felt so nice.

"So, your uncle seems kind of…scary," I admitted. It probably wasn't the best way to start out a conversation, but it was the first thing that came to me.

Leo laughed. At least he wasn't

offended by it. "Yeah, he likes it when people are scared of him. He's actually a nice guy. He took me in when I was little, and he's done well by me so far."

"Do you mind if I ask what happened to your parents?" Might as well get the tough subjects out of the way.

Leo stared at the ground. "They died in a car accident when I was little. Uncle Dev took me to live with him after that."

I thought about this for a minute. I love my Aunt Mallory, but I couldn't imagine living with her. My parents made me mad today, but I still loved them. Even if I wasn't about to admit that to them right now. I played with my necklace and frowned at the ground.

"What's wrong?" Leo asked.

"Oh, uhm…nothing. I'm sorry." I shook my head. "You reminded me of my parents. They did something awful today and... jeez, here I am mad at my parents and you're telling me how you lost yours. That must've been awful. I can't imagine…"

"It's okay. I still miss them all the time, but I had to move on. Uncle Dev's been great. He's helped me get through the rough patches." His smile was sad, and I reached over to hold his hand.

We sat there like that for a few minutes, each of us lost in our own thoughts. So much for getting to know each other. Just as I was about to try to start some small talk, he squeezed my hand.

"Wanna go for a run?" His eyes sparkled with mischief and made me want to be bad.

I smiled back. "Sounds like fun."

Chapter Nine

His body shimmered and became the beautiful golden wolf I remembered. I was awestruck and confused that I could think of a boy as 'beautiful.'

"Can I touch you?" I asked. I had an overwhelming desire to see if his fur was as soft as it seemed. I didn't have to wait long, because he came over and put his head underneath my hand.

His fur felt like a mixture of silk and wool. It was rough in some places, but when I dug my fingertips in, the fur near his skin was soft and downy. It was way longer than I'd originally thought, and I ran my fingers through and felt its soft roughness.

I could pet him for hours, but what I was doing was pretty much running my fingers through his hair. He wasn't even my boyfriend.

I blushed and stepped away. "Uh…thanks." I quickly shifted to my other form so he wouldn't see my embarrassment.

Looking over, I could swear he was smiling. Can wolves even smile? Sure, he's also a person, but I never thought that a wolf's long mouth could turn up in a grin like that. And yet, there it was.

He must be laughing at me, I thought and jumped into the forest. I was mortified. I couldn't believe I'd done that. I'd practically fondled him. I needed to run away, so I climbed the nearest tree.

Gazing down, I saw that Leo-wolf was staring up at me. He made a woofing sound and ran off. I watched him from my perch in the tree. He paused and woofed again. He still wanted me to run with him, despite my faux pas.

I climbed back down and ran for what seemed like hours. I darted between trees and jumped over underbrush. I climbed up a tree and stood on a branch, admiring the view. The freedom I felt in this new form was amazing. I felt like I could rule the world. I was amazed at the balance I had in this body. I was usually so clumsy. It was a nice change.

I thought about my parents, and how they'd taken away the only thing that used to bring me joy. I was happy I'd found something else that I loved, but I felt miserable at the thought that I may never be allowed to draw again.

My energy vanished at the thought.

Leo must have noticed I wasn't following him anymore, because he came back and put his front paws on the tree. He cocked his head at me, and woofed.

I climbed down the tree and changed back to myself again. I enjoyed the scenery from the ground for a second. The trees were closer together here, and the smell of sap permeated everything. The forest was quiet. The animals were probably afraid of the predators that had been stalking their home.

Leo shifted back and raised an eyebrow at me. "What's up? You need to head home or something?" He looked at the sky, like he was trying to figure out the time.

I shook my head. "No, I remembered why I was here in the first place. My parents...." I didn't know how to explain the hurt and betrayal I felt. I mean, it was only some art supplies. How could I explain to him what they meant to me? How could I possibly talk about my parents when he'd just revealed that he had none?

He gave me a small smile. "Big fight, huh? I get it."

I could tell he did. "Yeah, they invaded my privacy big time, and I'm not sure what to do about it."

"My advice?" He grabbed my hand with both of his and the tingling shot up my arm again. "Tell them how you feel. Uncle Dev has always-"

A black wolf shot through the trees and knocked Leo over. My hand immediately felt cold and I missed the tingles.

Leo rolled the wolf off him and sat up. "Uncle Dev! What are you doing?" Leo threw his hands out and yelled at his uncle.

The wolf stalked around us. He let out a low, menacing growl in my direction.

Leo stepped between the wolf and me. "Leave her alone, Uncle Dev. She didn't do anything."

On the one hand, this whole "gigantic growling wolf" thing was scary. On the other, Leo was ready to stick up for me. It was dreamy.

The wolf growled again, deep and

rumbling. Then, it shimmered and turned into Leo's uncle. He seemed taller than I remembered. Then again, maybe that's because I was cowering against a tree.

I stood up straight and took a step forward. I could be brave, as long as Leo was still standing between me and the scary guy.

"Leopold René Munroe, step away from that interloper this instant. I will dispose of her properly and you will go home." The alpha male's voice was loud and deep and scared me to death. Then I realized what he said. "Dispose of her." *Eep.* I hid behind Leo again.

"Don't do anything drastic. We were sitting here talking. No big deal, okay? Lay off."

Leo sounded authoritative, and oh-so-dreamy. But this wasn't the best time for that. This was the time for me to run home and hide under my bed. I'd never known anyone who was this intimidating. I didn't like it.

The big bad wolf rolled his eyes. "Leo, I

am not going to hurt her. I simply wish to escort her out of the woods. It is getting late and she really shouldn't be here. You know tha-"

His nostrils flared and his eyes darted over to me. "What are you?"

Suddenly, he was right in front of me. I wasn't sure how he did it, and I didn't want to think about it. Now, I really wanted to hide under my bed.

He took a deep breath. Then another. He sniffed me. It was weird. When he finally stopped, his eyes were blazing. "You are too young for a change. What are you? How have you changed already?"

This was one of those times when I didn't have any comeback handy. "I – I'm a panther." I didn't knowing what to say.

He leaned closer and I cringed. "Remarkable. How did this happen? Why? You are nothing but a child." He walked around me and I felt like I was a car he was inspecting for damage.

"My parents took me to a cave," I said quietly, not enjoying the 'child' comment, but too afraid to say anything confrontational. "They performed some weird ritual. I changed. I swear, I'm not here to cause trouble. I just want to go home."

Devereaux's gaze softened. He looked guilty. "I am sorry I frightened you, child. Please," he gently put his hand on my back and gestured to the path. "Let me walk you home. I wish to speak with your parents."

I glanced at Leo, who smiled supportively. Devereaux caught my glance and turned to glare. "Go home. We will speak of this when I return."

Leo nodded to him and gave me another small smile. It was supposed to reassure me. It didn't. He turned around and disappeared into the woods.

"Please, child, follow me." Devereaux

led me to the path and out of the forest. He kept glancing back at me to make sure I was following. Like I would go anywhere else. I was terrified he would change his mind and tear me apart. Nobody but Leo knew where I was, it would take forever for anyone to find me out here.

When we got to my house, I opened the front door and heard pots banging around in the kitchen, so I headed that way. I knew it wasn't Tony, because he never uses dishes for anything – he always eats straight from the can.

Mom was filling a pot with water. She turned around and was startled enough to drop it into the sink. She quickly recovered, wiping her hands dry on a towel.

"Mr. Munroe, to what do we owe this honor?" Mom held out a hand to the wolf. I had never seen her so nervous.

"Mrs. Brooks," Devereaux grasped her hand and shook it lightly. "I came to speak with you and your husband."

"Tessa, go get your dad. He's in the garage," Mom said. Her smile was a little too big. It had to be forced.

I hurried outside to get Dad. He was working on his 1957 Chevrolet Bellaire. He got a rusty old frame from a junk yard about two years ago and worked on it almost every day.

When I told him Devereaux Munroe was in the kitchen, he didn't even scrub his hands all the way clean before he ran inside. I followed slowly. I was in no rush to be in the middle of that conversation.

"I am concerned that you did not bring this to my attention immediately," I heard Leo's uncle say, when I reached the living room.

"We weren't sure how to contact you," Dad explained reasonably. "We didn't want to simply come to your house."

"No, quite right. I am relieved I found out as quickly as I did, then. This is a serious matter that requires serious discussion. What are we going to do with the girl?"

I stopped outside the doorway. I didn't want to interrupt. I didn't want to draw any attention to myself. What did he mean, *do with me?*

"*We* are going to teach her the same as normal," Dad responded. He didn't sound annoyed on my behalf, but he did make sure Mr. Munroe knew who was making the rules in this case. Go, Dad! "She'll be placed into an accelerated curriculum so she can learn everything we can teach her. We haven't been able to contact any of the elder societies to discuss the other matter, however-"

I had to assume the other matter was me being able to see the future. I had to let them know what I thought. I stepped into the kitchen. "It's fine, Dad. I don't want to learn anything about the visions. I haven't had anything happen today. I bet now that I've gone through the first shift, that part is sleeping or something. I won't use it." And that was that. Or not.

"Just because you went through one day without incident does not mean that your abilities are dormant. You must be trained to use them properly. You must be able to call on them at will," Devereaux said.

Of course, they would think they have a say in my life.

"Fine." I turned on Dad. "Then why did you take away all of my drawing stuff? If I'm going to be your prisoner, or your lab rat, why can't I have the one thing that I enjoy?"

Mom and Dad looked at each other and then down. They felt guilty? Good. They should. "You guys didn't even talk to me about it. You just did it. If you're going to control my entire life, you sure picked a great thing to start with."

I was getting fired up now. "Besides, if I wanted to draw, what's to stop me from drawing at Chloe's? Or going to the store and stealing supplies? You can't control me like that if you ever want me to do your bidding."

I was so mad now that I was shaking. My cheeks felt hot. I could feel tears start to well up in my eyes. Before they could fall down my cheeks, I turned and ran up the stairs to my room. Slamming the door, I threw myself on my bed. If they were going to treat me like I was five, without a mind of my own, I was sure going to act like it.

I could hear voices through the vents in my room, but I couldn't make out what they were saying. I could figure it well enough, though. They were probably talking about how I obviously couldn't handle any type of responsibility and they should lock me up until I am older and more mature. Like I would let that happen.

Then I had a horrible thought. What if the wolf shifters decided I was too much of a liability to them and they decided to off me?

That made my heart beat faster.

Shifting Dreams

Logically, I figured they wouldn't kill a kid. But it didn't stop my hands from sweating. I had to get out of there. I knew my parents wouldn't let me leave, so I didn't bother going down the stairs. I went to my window and pushed up.

The window didn't budge.

I pushed and pushed. I couldn't get it to move at all. I looked around and that's when I saw them. Small screws on either side of the window pane. They had locked me in my own room.

I was their prisoner.

Chapter Ten

I thought about my situation. My parents and a possibly homicidal wolf-shifter were downstairs, in the kitchen. My bedroom window was locked. What could I do? I had to come up with a plan.

I quickly shoved a couple sets of clothes into my backpack. There was nothing else in it since my jailers had taken away my art supplies. I had a couple of protein bars in my desk, so I grabbed those too. I quietly slipped out of my room, and closed the door behind me. I snuck down the hall to my parents' room. It was on the side of the house, so there was no tree for me to climb, but I figured I could find something to help me climb down.

Glancing out the window, I saw a fence,

about five feet from the end of the side roof. That was a long way to fall if I slipped, or misjudged the distance. That's when I remember, cats always land on their feet.

Slowly opening the window so I wouldn't make any noise, I put my backpack on the roof. I pulled myself up on the window sill and eased my body through the window. I crouched on the roof and I thought about my other form. I felt the tightening of my muscles and I lifted my paws. The backpack strap slid easily around my neck, like a collar. I was as ready as I could ever get.

I jumped.

My feet made a soft *fwomp* when I landed on the grass. That was way easier than I thought it would be. I shifted back, because I figured it was probably easier to sneak around the town as a human than a panther. Some kid would scream to their parents and my escape would be for nothing.

I glanced around to see if anyone was watching. I didn't even know where to go. I couldn't go to Chloe's. Her dad was the sheriff. He would bring me right back home. If I went to the woods, the wolf-shifters would be on me in a second. Leo told me he could smell me, and some of them probably had even better sniffers than he did.

Vin. I bet he would help me out, at least for a little while. He could probably hide me from his parents. They may not have been here long, but I was sure they would tell my parents where I was. Loyalty seemed to be a big thing around here, as long as you weren't some once-in-a-lifetime freak like me.

I headed in the direction of Vin's house. He lived in an older place on the other side of town, so I had kind of a long way to go on foot.

I ran at first, like I was someone out for a run, training for track or something. I figured sneaking around would only make people think I was doing something bad. When I got to the end of the block, I turned. I didn't want to be on my street longer than necessary. This way, if my parents walked outside, they couldn't look around and see me.

Changing direction a couple of times, I ran out of steam. I stopped and bent over, breathing heavily. I should have worked harder in gym class. I was out of shape.

I promised myself that I would start running every day if I made it out of this with my freedom. Of course, if I was going to be locked in a cage from now on like some lab rat, I might as well ask for a treadmill…or an exercise wheel.

Leaning over, I caught my breath and started to walk again. I still had about a mile to go and wanted to get there before anyone knew I was gone.

I walked and thought about my parents. Did I really believe they would do anything to hurt me? No. But what could they do if someone with authority decided they were going to take me? I couldn't imagine any way they could keep me safe from that. If the wolf-shifters or one of those 'elder societies' dad talked about wanted to do experiments or something, what could they do?

No, it was better if I could hide out until the whole thing blew over, or until I could figure out what they were planning. I didn't know how long Vin could keep me a secret, though. A couple of days maybe? A week, at most. After that... well, I wasn't sure what to do after that.

My only hope was that everyone would decide I could go home and never have to deal with these visions again. And I hope they made that decision fast. I was already beginning to miss my home and my normal life.

When I reached Vin's street, I stopped. I couldn't walk on the street. His parents might see me. I walked further and went into the alley. It was hard finding the right house from the back, so I went back to the street and counted.

Shifting Dreams

1…2…3…4…5. It was the fifth house down. I reentered the alley and counted down five houses.

I'd only been to Vin's house once, but I was pretty sure his bedroom was at the back of the house. Unfortunately, there were no trees back there for me to climb.

I sighed and shifted again. I didn't want to get into the habit of doing this all the time. I would have to get used to it if I was going to be on the run, though.

No. This whole thing would blow over. I just had to wait it out in safety.

I jumped, and had to scramble up the wood siding to make it to the roof. I examined my path and saw a couple of claw marks on the side of the house. I cringed, hoping nobody would notice them.

I snuck over to the window and peeked inside. Bingo. Vin had his back to me and was surfing the internet. I couldn't tell what was on the screen, but he was reading intensely. I lifted my paw – whoops. Still a panther. I shifted back and tapped on the window.

Vin jumped and turned around. He came over to the window to let me in. "Tessa, what are you doing here? How did you get up here? Ohmygosh! Did you come in your new form?"

"I ran away from home," I said. "I'm not sure what's going on, but my parents and the leader of the wolf-shifters are talking. I turned into a black panther, and they're trying to decide what to do with me. I need to hide out. Can I stay here for a while?"

"A black panther? Sweet." He grinned and turned to the door. "Yeah, you can stay here. Let me tell Mom we're four for dinner."

"No! You can't tell them anything! Weren't you listening? I need to hide out here for a while until-"

"Why do you need to hide out? It kind of sounds like your parents are trying to help you. I don't get it," Vin interrupted again.

It was annoying, but I had to finish. "Okay, stop talking for a minute." I took a deep breath and let it out. "Yes, my parents said that I would die if I didn't change early. So, they supposedly saved me from that. But the wolf-shifters found out about it and now their leader is talking to my parents about what they're going to do with me. I'm worried that they will try to take me away and do experiments or something. I need somewhere to hide until I know if it's safe to go home!"

I paused and took a couple of deep breaths. Vin was studying me like he was trying to process what I told him. "Oh, okay. No problem. My parents are cool. Besides, I'm sure Dad already knows you're here. Come on."

We walked downstairs and into his kitchen, where his mom was making dinner and his dad was reading the paper.

"Hello, Tessa." Vin's dad smiled at me.

"I see you found a way to sneak into my son's room. Let's not make a habit of that, okay?"

"Yes, sir."

"Mom, Dad, is it okay if Tessa stays here for a few days? There's this whole thing going on and she needs us to be Switzerland."

His parents both nodded, like they knew what that meant. "Of course, sweetie," his mom said. She waved a set of tongs in the air and smiled. "Do you like fried chicken?"

This was all so weird. I didn't know what to say, but that didn't seem to matter, because Vin pushed me to the table and made me sit.

Before I knew it, there was a plate full of chicken and peas in front of me and a basket full of steaming hot rolls in the center of the table.

My stomach growled and I remembered how hungry I was. I managed to wait until everyone sat and Vin started eating before I took a bite.

"This is delicious, Mrs. Greyson. Thank you," I said. Nobody could ever say my parents didn't teach me manners.

"Thank you, Tessa. I rarely get verbal compliments," she smiled. "These two rarely take a breath between bites. Conversation doesn't generally happen around dinner time, except when we have guests."

"Yeah, I noticed Vin's way of eating. He kind of...shovels." I watched him use a roll to scoop a giant bite of chicken and peas.

He stopped halfway to his mouth. "What? I'm hungry." He shrugged and shoved the food in his mouth. He chewed a few times and pretty much swallowed a giant ball of slightly flattened food.

Vin's mom sighed and shook her head. "I've tried so hard, but I haven't figured out a way to fix it. So," she smiled at me, "what brings you to our table?"

I stared at my plate. I had forgotten about everything for a few minutes, and it was great. It was apparently time to remember and start dealing with it. I took a deep breath. I didn't want these people to look at me like everyone else did whenever they heard my story. But they were being so nice and open and honest, I figured they deserved to know what they were hiding.

"I'm a freak," I said. Vin's mom opened her mouth like she was going to protest. "No, I am. I...see things. I had some dreams, I drew a picture. They were all about the future. So, my parents forced my change early, and now the wolf-shifters are...threatening me I guess. It's this whole big thing and I don't know if it's safe to be home. Thank you both so much for letting me stay here while I figure this out."

Running out of breath, I had to sit there and focus on sucking air into my lungs. I glanced at the two parents and they both had blank expressions. They looked at each other and seemed to have some sort of mental conversation, because they both turned back to me and smiled.

"You can stay here tonight, dear," Vin's mom said. "But you need to go to school tomorrow."

"But-" I protested.

"No, Tessa. You need to go to school. I will call your mom and see how things are going over there," Vin's mom interrupted. "As a mother myself, I would want to know my baby is safe."

She glanced fondly over at Vin and frowned. He had green pea juice dribbling down his chin.

Great. Apparently this wasn't my best idea. My parents would know where I was, so if they did decide to let the wolf-shifters have at me, they wouldn't need to search for me. There was nothing I could do about it now. I had spent too much time here already, and they would already be searching for me if I tried to run now.

We finished dinner and I helped Vin clean up. His mom went into the living room and I heard her talking. She was probably calling my mom to tell her where I was.

"Sorry, Tessa. I thought they'd be cooler about this," Vin said.

"No, it's okay. I don't know how far I could have gotten before they caught me anyway." I had some time to think about it over the rest of dinner. "Those wolf-shifters have an amazing sense of smell. They would've gotten me before I hit the other side of Denver."

We finished the dishes in silence. I had to come up with a plan, in case the worst happened. I needed a good defense. I'd always heard that the best defense was a good offense, so that was probably a good place to start.

An idea formed in my head. Vin showed me the guest room and I got ready for bed. I borrowed one of his mom's pajama sets and sat up late. I listened for any unusual sounds, in case anyone tried to get me in the middle of the night. I figured out what I would do the next day. I finally fell asleep at three o'clock.

I was full of energy the next morning, which was a good thing. I threw on a loose grey cotton t-shirt over a purple cotton tank top and a pair of cotton jeans. Then I ran down the stairs to the kitchen.

Vin's mom was there and she pointed to a cupboard, which was apparently where the cereal was stored. Vin came in as I sat to eat. He grabbed a big mixing bowl and poured his cereal into that. That boy could eat. I wondered again why he didn't weigh a million pounds.

We walked to school and I laid out my plan.

"That's a great idea, Tessa," Vin said when I finished. "There is no way they can touch you."

I was glad he thought so, because we

were at school. I went to my locker and threw my backpack in. I didn't have any supplies anymore, so it's not like it would be useful to me anyway. I walked into homeroom as the bell rang. Everyone turned to watch me. Now was the time to put my plan into action.

    I took a deep breath and changed into a panther.

Chapter Eleven

The whole classroom was silent, and then I heard someone clap. It was Chloe. I was so glad she didn't seem to be mad at me. She'd had to walk to school alone this morning and I hadn't warned her in advance. I owed her some chocolate.

The rest of the class cheered and clapped and hollered. I waited a minute or so before I changed back to me again. I couldn't stop the smile I felt growing on my face. My cheeks felt warm, but I didn't care that much. *Try doing anything to me now. Everyone has seen me and now they all know what's up. Nobody can get away with making me disappear.*

"All right, class! That's enough! That's

enough!" Mrs. Britten tried to get the classroom under control. She was also trying hard to look angry and stern, but she turned to me and winked, so I knew that she approved of my display.

I went to Chloe and hugged her. "Sorry about this morning. I'll explain later."

She smiled. She knew I had a good reason for missing our walk together. I was so lucky she was my best friend.

Mrs. Britten gave up taking verbal attendance because of the noise level. When the bell rang, everyone rushed out of the classroom to tell everyone about the stunt I'd pulled. Mrs. Britten pulled me aside before I left. "Don't worry, Tessa. You are in great hands here. I don't know anyone in this town who would let anyone harm you." She smiled and I knew she meant it. I thanked her and walked to the next class with Chloe.

The rest of the day was a whirlwind. I

had so many people I didn't even know come up to me and ask me to change. I didn't, but it didn't matter. Someone had taken a video of me changing back to human and sent it around the school, so everyone knew that the rumors were true.

The day ended and I walked out of the building. I was glad for the walk home to prepare myself for the extreme grounding my parents would give me.

But apparently I wasn't going to be that lucky. Dad was parked out front and saw me before I saw him. He looked mad. He made a phone call and Mom appeared a minute later from around the corner. I guess they had covered the entrances so I couldn't get out without one of them seeing me.

I took a deep breath and held my head high. I was prepared for battle. They wouldn't punish me without hearing what I had to say for myself. That was for sure.

I didn't even make it to the car before Mom ran over and hugged me. "Honey, we were so worried. Don't ever do that again!"

I was shocked. I expected to be slapped in handcuffs and taken immediately to my room, where I would never see the light of day again. "I'm sorry, Mom."

"I'm glad you're safe. You're grounded for a month." There it was.

"How about a week?" I asked. I could usually convince them to downgrade my punishments. Especially since I wasn't the one who was normally in trouble.

"Two weeks, and don't push your luck," Dad said. He came over and hugged me too. He kissed my forehead. "You have some explaining to do."

I nodded. Of course, they wanted to know why I'd left. Deep down, I always figured they wouldn't let anything happen to me. But I haven't exactly been in my right mind the last couple of days.

"Let's go home," Mom said, still holding on to me. "You can explain over pie."

Mom always baked when she was upset. Usually, she started with cookies, moved to bread, and then went to pie as a last resort. She must have been really upset if there was pie at home. Now I felt bad.

We got home and sat around the kitchen table. Mom served pie, and I picked at it. I didn't know where to start. "I'm sorry, guys. I don't know what I was thinking."

"You were probably thinking Mr. Munroe was going to gobble you up and spit you out." That was Mom, knowing exactly what to say, and being right on about how I thought. When she put it like that, I felt like an idiot.

"Yeah, I guess I was," I said. "He is really scary. I thought he might talk you guys into doing something awful. I wasn't going to leave for good. I wanted to be sure."

"We know, honey," Mom said. "When we got the phone call from Mrs. Greyson, we were going to come straight over and bring you home."

"But I convinced your mother that we all needed some time to calm down," Dad said. "Now that we have, we need to stick together. This is new for all of us, and I think we all need to support each other. The next few years are going to be hard on everyone. We will try to be fair with you, but you need to be fair with us. You need to talk to us about what you're feeling so we can help you out."

I felt a giant weight lift off my chest. "Okay, I can do that."

I finally felt better, so I took a bite of pie. Cherries burst in my mouth. Sweet and tart and perfect. I hated that Mom was upset, but I sure did love the results.

We ate our pie in silence until Dad's phone rang. He glanced at the number and immediately went to his office and shut the door. I could hear his voice through the wall, but I didn't know what he was saying.

When he came back to the kitchen, he seemed relieved. "That was Elder Bruin," he said. I had no idea who that was, but I figured he was important. "Apparently, there is someone who can help you with your ability. She will be here tomorrow. She has about a week that she can spare for you right now."

"What do you mean? I thought I was the first one in like, decades, or something." I was confused.

"About a century, actually. This person, Nadine, studies parts of our history that aren't in the normal textbooks. She knows something about," he waved at me, "whatever is going on here."

"Oh." Great, so some old lady thought she could tell me how to control my…powers, visions, whatever. I sighed. At least I would have something to do after school since I was grounded.

I left the kitchen to go to my room when Mom called me back. "Here, honey." She gave me my pencils and notebooks back. "You need to do your homework. You're right. We should have talked to you about it before we took your things. Only…please try not to draw anything until we figure this out, okay?"

I didn't want to have any more visions, so I had to agree. "I'll just do my homework for right now. Promise."

I took my things up the stairs and opened my bedroom door. The bear on my bed growled and swiped at the air. "Not now, Tony. I need to do my homework." I kicked the bear's leg and it growled again and shimmered back to Tony.

"Seriously, Squirt. This is going to happen."

I rolled my eyes at him and pushed him

out into the hallway. He was such a pain.

I did my homework and went to bed. I didn't have any dreams. I didn't wake up with a headache. This was how life should be.

School the next day was the same as the day before, except I didn't have nearly as many people ask me to change. I was no longer the center of the rumor mill, and I couldn't be happier about it.

I expected to come home to a strange car in the driveway, but there wasn't one. Maybe the lady, Nadine, wasn't supposed to get here until later. I dropped my bag inside the door and went to the kitchen for a snack. But, instead of walking into an empty room, I walked directly into the backside of a 200 pound gorilla.

I backed away quickly and thought to myself, *Surely, this wasn't a real gorilla, it had to be a shifter.* Maybe it was the infamous Nadine, although why she sat in the middle of our kitchen floor in the form of a gigantic gorilla, I had no idea.

It hadn't moved, except to turn around and watch me, so I took that as a sign that it probably wasn't a wild animal. "Are you Nadine?" I pressed my body against the wall and slid around to the front of it.

It cocked its head, and then nodded. I let out a breath that I didn't know I was holding. "Nice to meet you, I'm Tessa Brooks," I said, waving. "Sorry I walked into you. I didn't see your car."

It was one thing to talk to Tony when he was bear-shaped. He was my brother. I knew him. I also knew he wouldn't hurt me. This was a whole other thing. From what I knew about gorillas, I definitely didn't want to be on the wrong side of a fight with one. They could tear me apart, even in my other form. So, to say I was intimidated was probably an understatement. But, what could I do?

"I was going to get a snack. Would you

like something? We have apples, cookies, bread. My mom also made some pie." I rifled through the cupboards and fridge. "I know it's here somewhere."

"No, thanks. I am not hungry."

I turned around and saw one of the most beautiful women I'd ever met. Nadine was definitely not old, like I'd thought she would be. She had long, brown hair that she'd put back in a loose ponytail. She had big brown eyes and pouty red lips. Her cheekbones stood out, and her skin was perfectly smooth. She looked like she had stepped off the pages of a fashion magazine. Except for the fact that she had no style whatsoever. Her clothes were totally mismatched and too baggy, probably hiding an amazing figure.

"It is not polite to stare." She lifted a perfectly-manicured eyebrow.

"I'm sorry," I said, tearing my gaze away. "You're just not who I expected."

"You assumed I was a monstrous old lady," she said. It wasn't a question. "I get that a lot. Not many nineteen-year-olds walk into the archives to study history."

Nineteen? I examined at her clothes again and shrugged. "Water?" I asked, pouring myself a glass.

"Yes, that is what that is."

I rolled my eyes.

She laughed and pointed to a red water bottle on the counter. "Thanks. I have some. I know all about the dangers of altitude sickness."

Well, that's good. I didn't want to have to deal with anyone fainting or throwing up in front of me.

"So how did you get into history?" I didn't care, but I figured small talk was better than silence. I didn't know what else to say to this girl.

"That does not matter," she waved her

hand like she was waving off a fly. "We need to start right away with your training. I do not have much time, and we need to get everything under control."

"Oh, okay." I wasn't sure what to do.

Apparently, that wasn't a problem. "Tell me about everything that has happened so far, and we will go from there."

I told her all about the drawing of Leo's face before I even met him. I told her about the dreams. She seemed especially interested in the ones I'd had about Tony, his broken leg and how I knew that he would shift into a bear.

"That is interesting," she said. "Most of the records indicate that past Oracles could not see the futures of those closest to them."

Oracle? That word seemed so ancient and weird, especially when describing me. I made a face, but she didn't notice. She'd gone over to a bag by the back door that I hadn't seen and took out a notepad and pen. She scribbled furiously for a few minutes before she remembered I was there. "Oh, sorry. I am trying to get all of this down so I can get it into the books."

She put her pen down and stared blankly at me for a minute. It seemed like her mind was somewhere else completely. Her eyes cleared. "Okay, then. It is not practical to test the dreams, so we will start with the drawings."

She rifled through her bag and pulled out a sketch pad and a pencil. She put them on the table in front of me and stared expectantly.

"Uh…what do you want me to do?"

She jumped, like she didn't expect me to talk or something. "So sorry. I guess you have not forced them before." She thought for a second. "Okay, let us move to the living room. We are not sure what is going to happen." She mumbled to herself as she walked to the living room. Apparently Mom and Dad had welcomed a Crazy Pants into the house. Great.

Shifting Dreams

I walked into the living room with the pad and pencil in my hand. Nadine sat on a cushion in the middle of the living room. There was another cushion in front of her. I guess I was supposed to sit on the floor.

After I got settled, shefinally decided to explain what she wanted. "Okay, what I want is for you to think about somebody that you know, but not one of your friends or family. Let me know when you have picked someone."

I thought about it. Obviously, Chloe was out. I thought of Mrs. Britten. "Okay, got it. My teacher, Mrs. Britten."

She pointed to the pad and pencil in my hand. "Okay, open that up. Close your eyes and think about your teacher. Think about who she is. Think about anything she has ever said to you."

I sat there with my eyes closed for a few minutes. Nothing happened. I opened my eyes and saw that Nadine watched me. I figured I'd give her a show. I gasped and started to draw. I drew legs first, four long legs that ended in hooves. The body was big and the neck was long. I finished off my giraffe with some partially-shaded spots and a pair of glasses on the end of the long nose.

It was the first thing that I'd thought when I saw Mrs. Britten for the first time. It wasn't half-bad. I passed it over to Nadine and she scrunched her nose up when she saw it.

"Is this what you saw?" She shrugged. "I guess you might have the ability to know peoples' shapes. I never read about anything like that, but maybe the powers have been diluted over so many years."

She seemed disappointed when she handed the sketch pad back to me. "Okay, go ahead and try someone close to you. One of your friends."

I closed my eyes and thought about Chloe. I imagined her curly red hair, the freckles across her super pale face. I thought about her wearing her black Van Halen fitted shirt and jeans. She was so short....

The vision hit me like a brick.

The scream cut through the air like a siren.

We were frantically running, but we couldn't see anything. Were we running around in circles? There was no way of telling. It was so dark.

We tripped and fell, our hands shooting out in front of us to catch our fall. Something was here. It was right here, but we couldn't see it. Nothing but darkness. Nothing but-

"Ohmygosh! What was that?" My head felt the same way my stomach did whenever I was on an elevator.

I looked at my sketch pad. I had drawn the part where we had fallen. There was a ring on the right ring finger on the hands that had caught us. I knew that ring. It was the ring I gave

Chloe for her birthday last year. That meant-

"What is wrong? What is it?" Nadine grabbed the paper from me and studied it. Her eyebrows pulled together and she tilted her head. "This does not appear to be an animal."

"It's not. Okay, that last one, with Mrs. Britten, I was messing with you. This time, I actually saw something, like I was dreaming."

I took a deep shaky breath. I looked at my trembling hands and felt tears well up in my eyes. "I think I saw...I think Chloe is in danger. She was running from someone, something. I don't know." I choked up and I couldn't talk anymore.

What had I just seen? Had I really seen my best friend being murdered?

Chapter Twelve

Nadine got up and ran into the kitchen. She came back with a phone in one hand and my glass of water in the other.

I sipped at the water, which helped me start to breathe normally again.

"Mrs. Brooks? Hello, this is Nadine." She paused. "Yes, thank you. Listen, I need you to come home right away. I am not sure what is going on, but Tessa needs you right now. I-"

She stopped talking and held up her phone. "She hung up." She took my free hand in hers. Either her hands were burning up or mine were freezing.

Images ran through my mind over and over again. I couldn't get them to stop. I stood up and went to my bag. I grabbed my phone and dialed up Chloe. When she answered, I heaved a sigh of relief. "I'm so glad you're safe. Chloe, listen. You need to call your dad. Tell him you need him to come home."

"What's going on, Tessa? Are you in trouble?"

"No, I'm not. Just do it, please? I need to make sure you're okay. You guys can come over when he gets there, but don't leave the house without him!"

There was a pause on the other end, until I heard her agree and hang up. I suddenly had no energy and I collapsed in the middle of the floor. Nadine rushed over to make sure I was okay.

My muscles were weak and I could barely hold my eyes open. I'd never felt this tired in my life. I needed to sleep for a few minutes…

***

When I opened my eyes, I was laid out on the couch.

Mom stood over me with her stethoscope, listening to my chest. She smiled and ran her fingers across my forehead. "You had me worried, sweetheart. How do you feel?" She held her hand against my forehead, like she used to do when I was little and had a cold.

"Tired." I tried moving my legs, but they still felt weak. I could lift my arm, but when I tried to pick up the glass next to me, I dropped it and sloshed a couple drops of water on the table. "How long was I out?"

"You were unconscious for almost an hour." Nadine's face peeked over the back of the couch. "When your mom got home, we moved you to the couch."

"What happened?" I stretched. I felt a bit more awake.

"You passed out." Nadine was apparently Miss Obvious.

"When I got home, you were laying there, sleeping. I couldn't find anything wrong, so I had to sit here and wait," Mom said. She was clearly worried, and she listened to my breathing and heartbeat some more. "I called your dad. He should be home soon."

"I don't get it. Why did I pass out? I don't-" I remembered my vision, or whatever it was. "Chloe! Is she okay?"

I tried to sit up but Mom pushed me back. "Calm down, honey. Chloe's dad called me. He told me that he is home with her now. I will let him know they should come over once your dad gets home." She ran her hand across my forehead again. "Just rest, okay? You scared me. I need to make sure you're okay before I let you get up."

It was nice to have Mom taking care of me like she used to. I sipped my water and saw the sketch pad still on the floor. Nadine caught my gaze and brought it over to me.

Shifting Dreams

There weren't very many details, and I already couldn't remember everything that happened in my vision. I decided that's probably what it was – a vision of the future. I had trouble wrapping my mind around that. The drawing was just two hands. There was nothing there that could help us figure out when or where this was supposed to happen.

A bottle of something was suddenly shoved in front of my face. I checked it out and turned to Nadine, who watched me expectantly.

"Super Muscle Juice? Isn't this the stuff that body builders drink? No, thanks. I'm good," I tried to hand it back to her but she didn't take it.

"You need it to keep your energy up. Trust me. You passed out earlier because your precognition took so much out of you. Unless you want to spend the rest of your life in a bed, you will learn to love that stuff."

I opened it, took a sip, and gagged. "I

will never learn to love this." But I gulped the rest of it down. When I finished, I gulped the rest of my water, too. I could still taste chalk. I had to brush my teeth.

I sat up and tried to stand. I was expecting to feel dizzy still, but it wasn't too bad anymore. I looked at Nadine. "Thanks. I guess I needed that."

She followed me when I walked to the bathroom to brush my teeth and rinse that nasty taste out of my mouth. I was glad that I had an extra toothbrush in the downstairs bathroom. I didn't think I could climb those stairs quite yet.

"I'm a big girl, I can brush my own teeth," I said to her when I reached the bathroom.

"I am sure," she said. "But I am here in case you can no longer stand. So suck it up and do what you need to do."

She stood against the door frame and watched me. I shrugged and got my toothbrush ready. Halfway through, I had to sit on the toilet to finish brushing. Nadine didn't say anything, but I could tell from her expression that she wanted to say *I told you so.*

We walked back to the living room where I sat back on the couch with a sigh. It felt good to be resting again. The front door opened and Chloe ran in, followed by her dad. He was still in his uniform.

"I'm so glad you're okay," I said when Chloe sat. I gave her a hug.

"Of course, I'm okay," she said. "What's this all about?"

Mom brought Mr. McEvoy over and he sat on a chair across from me. I didn't know where to start, but Mom had my back.

"Tessa had a vision of the future," she said.

"Or at least, one possible future," Nadine interrupted. Mom nodded for her to continue, so she did. "Tessa's precognitions, or visions, are not always going to be exactly correct. From what I have read, they are based on what is happening now. Once she has a vision, we can make any possible number of decisions that may change the course of the future."

Huh? What did she mean? Every vision I'd had before has come true like I'd seen it.

"What do you mean, Miss…?" Mr. McEvoy asked. He looked confused, and I couldn't blame him. I still wasn't sure what was happening.

"Nadine," she said. "Tessa saw something happen to someone who she thinks is her friend, Chloe. Now that we know there is a danger, we are going to take necessary precautions. Once we have done that, we have changed the course of the future. So the danger might still be around, but it has changed."

Mr. McEvoy frowned thoughtfully. His thick reddish blond eyebrows scrunched together. His big moustache moved from side to side while he considered what Nadine had told him.

I had a question. "So, what, now that we know she's in danger, we keep her safe, and she's not in danger anymore?"

"More or less. She may not be in any danger anymore, the danger might lessen, or it may move to someone else. It is hard to tell with these kinds of things."

"What do you mean, move to someone else?" I was getting worried about the rest of my friends now.

Nadine made a face and thought about it for a minute before responding. "Say the danger is a kidnapper, which is what it sounds like from your description. If Chloe is protected, the kidnapper may decide it is not worth it and moves on. Or he could decide to grab someone who is not nearly as well-protected, like another kid. He could even decide that the danger to *him* is too great and he decides not to take anyone at all."

"I like that last option," Chloe said. She was curled up at the end of the couch. She shivered and I moved closer to her and grabbed her hand. This was a lot for both of us to handle.

Mr. McEvoy stood up and turned to my mom. "Eva, if it's okay, I'd like to leave Chloe with you for right now," he said. She agreed and he turned to us. "Stay here. Stay inside. I'm going to alert the force that there is a possible kidnapper in the area."

"Is there anything else I can do?" Mom asked.

"Yes, call Doris and tell her what's going on. It's probably the fastest way to spread the word and get kids inside and safe."

Mom's receptionist, Doris, was a wonderful woman and I loved her like a grandmother. She was also the biggest gossip in town. You never told her anything that you didn't want everyone to know. It was a good plan.

Mr. McEvoy kissed Chloe and thanked my mom again. When he left, Mom locked the door behind him and looked around anxiously. "You girls go upstairs and do your homework. Nadine, can I get your help in the kitchen? I'm going to call Nora and let her know her daughter is with us. She'll probably want to come over and we may as well feed them all."

Nadine followed Mom to the kitchen and I slowly made my way up the stairs. Chloe followed my slow butt and we both flopped onto my bed.

"Man, what a week," I said. "Two weeks ago, we were just a couple of girls."

"Yeah," Chloe said. "And now we're hiding out from a kidnapper or whatever. This is crazy."

She turned to me. Her cheeks were flushed and her eyes were wide and wild. "I wonder if you can catch the bad guy!"

"What? Are you nuts?" I smacked her arm. "Your dad is going to find him. That's his job, remember?"

"Well, yeah. But how cool would it be if you were the one who solved the case? I mean, what if we can make your power work that way, you know? What if you could help solve crimes and stuff?" She was excited now, and she bounced on the bed while she talked.

"I don't want to solve crimes, Chloe!" I was tired again, and all I wanted was to take another nap. I wondered if Nadine had another bottle of that nasty protein stuff. "I want to be normal."

"But you're not normal, you big dweeb!" She noticed my face and apologized. "Look, I'm sorry. But you're not normal. You know it. Why not embrace it and do some good?"

I rolled my eyes, but I thought about it.

Shifting Dreams

She did have a point. I wasn't normal. I would never be normal again. I didn't have to solve crimes and prevent them and whatever all the time, but I could do it this once. Maybe. If I could make myself do that weird trance-thing again.

I took a deep breath. "Fine. But we'll do it tonight, after everyone's gone to bed. I'm too tired to try again right now."

Chloe squealed and bounced on the bed even harder. So, I pushed her off. She made a satisfying thud when her butt hit the floor.

We hung out and did our homework until Mom called us downstairs for dinner. I thought I was finally starting to feel like myself again. I didn't actually feel better until after my second helping.

Chloe made a face at me. "T, you're going to get so fat if you keep that up."

"Shut up. You try channeling the Woo Woo to see the future. See how hungry you are after." I stuck my tongue at her.

After dinner, Chloe and I convinced her parents that she should stay there overnight. It was a school night, but Mr. McEvoy was finally convinced when Mom offered to have Mrs. McEvoy stay in a guest room while he worked.

We ran up the stairs and closed my bedroom door. "Okay, so how do we do this?" Chloe asked as soon as she heard the door click shut.

"Well, last time I was sitting down and I had a pencil and paper," I said. I gathered my things and sat against the wall. I closed my eyes and thought about Chloe.

"Is something supposed to happen?" Chloe asked after about five minutes.

I opened my eyes and shrugged. "I dunno. Maybe you're no longer in danger, like Nadine said. I guess we can't help out after all." I wasn't actually that upset about it. I didn't want to go through that again.

"What if you thought of the kidnapper instead of me?" Chloe suggested.

I thought about it for a minute and shrugged. *What could it hurt?* I closed my eyes and thought about the kidnapper. I imagined myself chasing after Chloe.

The sound was overwhelming. Students were clapping and screaming as the cheerleaders in the center of the room riled them up. They were jumping and flipping and getting in the way of what we wanted to see.

The girl sat in the bleachers across the gym from us. She was searching around for something, but couldn't find it.

She was nothing special, so why did she get the attention? Why weren't we given more importance in this place? We were so far superior, it didn't even seem fair to her. We needed to hone our skills. Where to start...?

"Ohmygosh!" I gasped and dropped the pencil to the floor. "What a creeper!"

Chloe grabbed the notebook from my hand and saw what I drew. She gazed at me curiously. "You saw yourself?"

I shook my head. It was so much worse than that. "No, whoever it was watched *me*. I was being targeted by this creep."

Chapter Thirteen

"How do you know someone was targeting you?" Chloe shook her head in denial. "I mean, there are lots of reasons someone could be staring. Maybe it's someone who wants to ask you out!"

I shook my head and sighed. "That's not what it felt like. The thoughts were a little jumbled, but it seemed like whoever it was didn't like me at all."

I grabbed the drawing from Chloe and studied it. There was no question the picture was of me. I had no idea why. I felt a fading sense of jealousy, but why would someone be jealous of me? Sure, I shifted early and I have this weird ability, but who would be jealous of that? Why would anyone want to be labeled a freak?

"Let's go to bed. There's nothing we can do about it right now." I glanced back at the drawing and closed the book. "It's not like I have anything to give to your dad. The vision was pretty much a bust."

Chloe still appeared worried. "I guess. Except now we know that you're also in some kind of danger."

I thought about that for a minute. "We'll have to stick together." I yawned. I wasn't quite as tired after this vision, but I was definitely ready for sleep. "We'll tell Vin tomorrow. I'm sure he'll help watch out for us. It's not like anything will happen when we're in a group."

She gave me one last worried smile and we got into bed. Grateful for my queen-sized mattress, we curled up side-by-side and went to sleep. Things couldn't possibly be as bad as they seemed.

***

I was so wrong. I stared at my closet in horror. Why, oh why, did I have to buy so many new clothes that were *not* my style? What in the world was I thinking? Standing there in my towel, my hair dripping wet from the shower, I couldn't do anything but stare.

In the logical part of my mind, I knew they all fit. Emotionally, I wasn't even close to picking out something to wear.

After yesterday's nasty vision, I was sure everyone would know about my abnormality. Add to that the fact that my mom was dropping us off at school an hour early, and I knew everyone would be staring at me. I didn't want anyone thinking I was a freak *and* a fashion disaster.

I groaned and threw myself on my unmade bed. I was considering whether or not I could successfully fake being sick when Chloe came in, hair wet from her shower, wearing her signature black jeans and a vintage red and black halter.

"You're not dressed yet? Tessa, we have to leave in like, twenty minutes. You know it takes you longer than that to do your hair!" She rifled through my clothes and threw a pair of

Capri jeans and a cute green cap-sleeved v-neck on the bed next to me. "Get dressed. I'll see you downstairs."

After she left, I scrutinized the outfit she'd picked out for me. I could do worse. I threw the clothes on, brushed my hair up into an easy ponytail and added a pair of silver hoop earrings. I had enough time to grab a quick breakfast before Mom ran us out the door.

The school was still deserted when we got there. Of course, Mrs. Mintz, the principal was there. She sat in her office next to the commons area, door open and not-so-casually watching over the couple of students that were there early.

Chloe and I sat against a wall and played with a deck of cards. Kids were shuffling in a little at a time. Apparently, word had gotten around and none of the other parents were taking any chances with a possible kidnapper on the loose.

Doris obviously hadn't left out the tiny detail that it was *my* vision. Whispers and ugly stares were thrown my direction, and I heard the words "freak" and "weird" more than once.

When Vin got there, Chloe and I were glad to have someone else to talk to. When it was just the two of us, it was hard to ignore the stares. With a third person, it was way less uncomfortable.

"Okay, seriously. I leave you alone for one day, and suddenly you're the school leper or something. What gives?" Vin sat and pulled a loaf of banana bread out of a foil packet and took a big bite directly from the end.

"I don't want to talk about it. Let's talk about you and your insane need to eat like, a million calories a day. Why don't you weigh a thousand pounds?" I was sick of explaining. I figured a distraction was in order. And it worked like a charm.

"Dunno. I've always eaten like this." Vin shrugged. "Mom thinks it's because I'm a guy. Dad thinks it's because my body's saving up because I'm going to be an elephant or something."

He put down his food long enough to make a trunk out of his arm and trumpet like an elephant. We all laughed. Gotta love Vin. Who else could make a joke when everyone was staring and whispering?

The thought stopped my laughter, and I noticed that people were leaving. It was almost time for class to start. I didn't think I could love first bell any more than I did right then. I kept hearing something that sounded a lot like the word "monster" and I was so happy for anything that would get me away from that.

When I felt the hand on my shoulder, I turned to see Mrs. Mintz, the principal. "Miss Brooks, please come with me."

I waved 'goodbye' to Chloe and Vin and followed her, red-faced, into the office. The door shut behind me. "Take a seat."

I sat in the only chair in front of the desk. "Am I in trouble?" I asked, worried.

"No, not at all. I wanted to give you

your new schedule." She picked up the only piece of paper on her desk and examined it. Satisfied that everything was in order, she passed it over to me.

I held it carefully, pinched between my fingers, like I was holding a squiggling spider. I glanced at my new class list. Everything had been moved around. I no longer had any classes, except Life Skills, with Chloe or Vin. I had the same lunch hour, but I no longer had the electives I'd been attending. My two art classes had disappeared, replaced by Life Skills 2 and Alteration Series 1.

I looked up at Mrs. Mintz. Before I could open my mouth, she explained. "We had to rearrange your classes so you could learn the skills necessary to shift safely and securely." She paused, letting this sink in. "I apologize for your missing art classes. There was no other way to fit the state-required classes into your schedule. You understand."

She stared at me, the corners of her mouth tilted down in a permanent frown. In the few times I'd seen her in the hallway, she always had this same expression, like she was constantly bored. She reached into a drawer to pull out a pen and a slip of paper.

She scribbled quickly and passed it over to me. "Here is your late pass. Please proceed directly to your first class. Mrs. Britten was already notified that you would be absent in Homeroom."

I took the paper and walked to the bathroom. I had no intention of going directly to my new Algebra class. I had a late pass, and I was going to use it to its fullest.

I stared at my reflection in the mirror and sighed. I'd never been able to hide my emotions – they were always easy to see on my face. My brown eyes were sad, my eyebrows tight and low. I tried smoothing them out with my hands. I couldn't go to class looking like a dejected loser.

I pulled out my lip gloss and applied a generous layer. The smell of cherries and chocolate filled my nose and I closed my eyes and took a couple of deep breaths. When I opened my eyes again, my features were more or less back to normal. If only I could breathe some normal into my life. I snorted. Like that would happen. I'd need to get through the morning without my best friends and try to ignore the stares and whispers.

I needed a miracle.

***

"Where were you all morning?" Chloe caught up with me as I walked into the courtyard. "You weren't in class. I was worried you'd gotten suspended or something!"

I hugged Chloe and held back frustrated tears. "No, I'm not in trouble. They rearranged my schedule. I'm never going to see you again this year, except in Life Skills. I'm now in two Life Skills classes and another class that I can only assume has something to do with shifting."

Chloe stuck out her tongue and made a face to let me know what she thought about this. I shrugged. Nothing either of us could do about it.

We headed over to the shady spot under our tree, but we stopped cold. Westy and a couple of his friends stood around the tree and talked. We turned around as fast as we could, but they had already spotted us.

"Hey, Freak Show!"

"Yeah! Hold up, Miss Cleo!"

We walked as fast as we could, but I felt a hand grab my arm and turn me around. I fell back and tripped on someone's foot. I landed hard on my butt. I looked up and saw the three faces mocking me.

"Watch it, klutz, or you're going to get caught by the bad, evil man!" That was Bruiser. His real name was Bobby, and I always thought he got the nickname from football. Apparently he was nothing but a jerk.

"Leave her alone, Jock Head!" Vin had caught up with us and pushed his way between me and the guys. He was half their size, but that didn't stop him.

"Or you'll do what, Twig? You gonna poke me with your scrawny elbow or something? Get out of the way and only your freak show girlfriend gets hurt." Bruiser shoved up against Vin and pushed his shoulders. Vin stumbled but caught himself before he fell.

The other guy, Jake, went to Vin's other side and grabbed him. Vin struggled, but Jake was a lot bigger and stronger. He wouldn't let go.

Bruiser sneered. "Too bad you picked a wuss for a boyfriend."

I thought about Leo and wished he was here. But no, I didn't need him to protect me. I was strong. The very same powers that these guys were harassing me for were the ones that were going to get us all out of this.

I'd had enough. I didn't have to put up with this. Staring and whispering was one thing, but I wasn't about to put up with anyone hounding me or my friends.

I threw my backpack, shimmered to my panther form, and yowled. The football guys' eyes went wide and Bruiser took a step back.

"Hey, we were only teasing. Things got outta hand. We'll leave you alone." Westy finally stepped forward, his hands spread in front of him like he was calming an angry lion. And in a way, he was. "We didn't mean any harm."

Right then, something hit on my back legs and knocked me over. I looked around and saw a horse standing there with its teeth bared.

"You didn't think we'd come to a shifter fight without a shifter, did you? You're stupider than you look!" Bruiser laughed.

Now I didn't know what to do. I didn't want to hurt anyone, just scare them a bit – remind them of what I can do.

If I turned around and hurt this guy, this horse, was I any better than them? I mean, there's a point where I should fight back. But was I in any real danger?

I looked at Vin, who looked angry. He was standing still, but I got the feeling he was waiting for some signal from me to start fighting again. Had I become the leader of our group? I didn't want the job.

I looked over at Bruiser, and saw that he was inching closer, like he was getting ready to tackle me. If he tackled me and hurt me, I would have to fight back. And a fight between a panther and a boy, even a big football player like him, would be a bloodbath.

But I couldn't stand there and take a beating. I knew I only had a few more seconds to decide what to do, and my mind raced.

Luckily, I didn't have to do anything. I spotted Tony at the same time he spotted me. He pushed his way through the crowd that had begun to gather.

"Problem, Westy?" he said with his hands balled into fists. "You're not messing with my little sister, are you?"

"Of course not," Westy backed away and gestured to the horse. "No problem here."

"I wonder if Coach Fillion will say the same when I ask him about this," Tony threatened. "I'm sure he'll be real interested to know that his JV quarterback picks on innocent little girls."

Westy narrowed his blue eyes and sneered. "Go ahead and tattle. You'll pay for it, Pooh Bear." He and his football buddies strutted away and the rest of the crowd went back to eating. When I was back in my own skin, Tony came over.

He looked me over and grinned. "You know, when you promised me a brawl, I figured it would be with me."

I had to smile. "Yeah, well, I figured it would be, too. Thanks, Tony."

"No problem, Squirt. You okay?" When I nodded, he squeezed my shoulder. "See ya later. I need to go talk to Coach."

Tony walked off. I stood there and stared at Chloe and Vin. I didn't know what to say. I'd never been in a situation like that before. Nobody ever paid enough attention to me to want to hurt me. At that moment, I was so glad that Chloe and I were never the type to make fun of anyone. And now I could say that I wouldn't let anyone else be treated like that, either.

My hands were still shaking when Chloe grabbed one. We walked inside with Vin and sat in the commons area. I was grateful for my friends, and the fact that Vin shoveled food in his mouth almost the second we sat down.

I opened my backpack and pulled out my lunch. It was smashed and inedible from when I'd thrown my bag. Great. I sighed and tossed it in the trash. When I came back, Vin held out a bag full of sandwiches.

"Mom always packs a lot. Help yourself." He smiled.

"Thanks. I'm starving."

We ate lunch mostly in silence. By the end of the hour, I felt better. I think Chloe and Vin did too, because they cracked jokes about my shift.

"So, if Tony is Pooh, does that make you Tigger?" Chloe asked, and we all laughed. The bell rang and we all went off to class. I couldn't wait until the end of the day, when I could finally have a class with Chloe and we could all go home. I was so tired of all the attention I was getting.

But things only got worse. During History, I was called to the principal's office. Again. This time, Mrs. Mintz wasn't the only one waiting for me.

Coach Fillion sat in a folding chair in front of the desk, his wide shoulders filling up half the room. I sat next to Coach, feeling nervous. I knew I hadn't done anything wrong, but it's the principal's office. I'd never been called there before, and here I was, the second time in one day.

"Miss Brooks," Mrs. Mintz came over and sat next to me.

I think she was trying to make me feel less nervous, but I was surrounded by authority and power on both sides. It was probably my imagination, but I could feel the energy. It made me shrink in my chair.

"Are you feeling all right, Ms. Brooks?" Mrs. Mintz looked at me with what was probably concern. "We heard about what happened earlier, and we need to know how you feel. Were you injured?"

I shook my head. "No, I'm fine."

Coach sighed and leaned forward. He was a big man, and instead of making him seem smaller and easier to talk to, leaning forward made it so he was all up in my personal space.

"Brooks, we're prepared to suspend those boys," Coach said. He shook his head. "It doesn't matter that we'll probably lose the rest of the season. I can't encourage that type of behavior from members of my team. All I need is a nod from you, and it's done."

So now it seemed that the future of the football team rested on my shoulders. Like that wasn't a lot to ask. Do adults even know what kind of pressure they put on us when they do things like that? If I nodded, half of our starting lineup would be gone and I would become more of an outcast. If I said no, I would probably be putting myself in a situation where they attack me again.

Finally, I sighed. "Look, Coach, Mrs. Mintz, I don't think they'll bother me again. Please don't make a big thing of this. Do what you want, but leave me out of it, please?"

They looked at each other and seemed to have a silent conversation. Coach stood up. "Okay, detention it is. Don't hesitate to let me know if any of my boys try anything again, got it?"

I nodded and he left. I was alone in the office with the principal. She stood up and sat behind her desk.

"Miss Brooks, in the future, please resist shifting in public. If anyone sees you, it could be terrible for our community." She stared me down and I shrunk even further in my seat.

"Yes, ma'am."

"You may go." She looked at her computer and dismissed me without another glance.

I walked out into the crowded halls. Great, I'd missed another class. Whatever. All I had left was Life Skills. As long as nothing else happened for the next forty-five minutes, I was peachy.

Chapter Fourteen

"Today we're going to partner up and use our observation skills in real time." Everyone looked around at their friends when Mr. Norris said this. The excitement quickly faded when he continued. "And I will be choosing the pairs. This is a lab, people, not social hour."

I rolled my eyes at Chloe. Everyone hated when teachers did things like this, so why did they keep doing it?

Mr. Norris picked up his class roster and started naming people. "Anderson, you're with Young. Bailey, with Whitman." Being completely original, he was choosing the partners from the top and the bottom of the list. *Oh no, that meant...* "Brooks, Westin…"

Shifting Dreams

He droned on until he'd named everyone, but my world froze. Of course, I was partnered with Westy. I looked across the room at him and shuddered. He wore a grin that could only be described as *feral.*

"Mr. Norris, can Tessa and I switch partners?" Vin came to my rescue. I didn't want him to have to deal with that slime ball, but I didn't want to find out what that look was supposed to mean.

"Mr. Greyson, if we start switching partners around, everyone will want to do so. You will work with Miss Nelson." He set the class list down and went to the board. He wrote the words *sight, smell,* and *sound* on the board. "You will use these senses today. Try to determine details about your partner that are not readily apparent.

"We can all see the clothes you are wearing. Go beyond that and describe your partner in as many details as possible. Try to determine what your partner may have been thinking when getting ready for school this morning, for class this afternoon. You have the remainder of the hour. Go."

I sat in my chair. No way was I going to move any closer to Westy, even if it meant I failed this assignment. He didn't seem to have the same thought. I was overwhelmed by the smell of cologne and arrogance when he came over.

"Partnered up, huh? Must be my lucky, lucky day." Westy pulled a chair entirely too close to me and sat, his shoulder brushing mine in the process.

I moved away. "Whatever. I'm stuck with you, so let's do this." I opened my notebook and clicked my pen open. *I need to get through the next,* I glanced at the clock, *forty-one minutes. I can do this.*

"Yeah, let's do this," he said as he leaned over my desk. "What would you like to do?"

My gaze shot up to his face and what I saw made me throw up in my mouth a little bit. "Just do the assignment and go away, Westy."

"Please, call me Arthur," he practically purred back.

"Only your girlfriends call you that. And I'm not your girlfriend." I leaned as far away from him as possible, but this only brought his attention lower, to my chest. I quickly moved back and put my notebook between us.

"Give it time, Kitten. Give it time." He leaned back and showed me his teeth. It was meant to be a grin, but it was way more predatory.

"Gross. Can we please do this assignment?" I gestured to Mr. Norris, who was watching us. "If I'm going to be stuck sitting next to you, the very least you can do is make sure I don't fail."

"Don't worry, Kitty Cat. Teachers don't fail me or mine. They know better."

The arrogance of this guy was irritating me. If he wasn't going to take this seriously, I'd do the assignment on my own and ignore him. Easier said than done, with him leering at me. I'd never been leered at. I didn't like it.

I managed to scribble down a few things, including *arrogant, jerk,* and *sleaze ball.* The last bell rang and I turned my paper in and rushed out the door.

Tony and Mark were leaning against some lockers in the hallway, talking. They noticed me and straightened up, ready to follow me home.

"I don't need protecting, Tony," I said. I felt better knowing he was there, but I also felt embarrassed that he thought I needed a shield or something.

"I'm not protecting. I'm walking here with my buddy. Don't mind us." They fell back and talked. I couldn't hear their words, but they were probably discussing football.

I rolled my eyes and waited for Chloe. Secretly, I was grateful for Tony being there. Especially when Westy strolled out and gave me a long stare, from head to toe and back up again.

Chloe bumped into him as she walked

out of the class and made him lose eye contact. She grinned at me, letting me know that it wasn't an accident. "My dad told me to go home with you today. He said he'll pick me up whenever he gets done with his shift." She pulled me down the hall.

"Great, you can help me with math," I said. She knew how awful I was with numbers, so she didn't even pause before nodding.

We walked home, Tony and Mark following about a block back. Westy drove past us at one point. He was going slowly, and he stared me down, but at least he didn't say anything.

"What is with him?" Chloe said as he squealed his tires ahead of us. "First, he and his clones attack you at lunch, and now he's hanging all over you?"

I shrugged. I had no idea what his deal was. "He seems to think that I'm suddenly interested in being his girlfriend. I dunno. I don't want to think about it. It's all way too creepy."

Chloe grabbed my arm and stopped me. "Hey! Do you think that maybe he's the person you saw in that vision? Maybe he's the one being all Grandmaster Creepster!"

I thought about it. "Maybe."

We walked the rest of the way in silence. The guys were laughing behind us, but I couldn't hear what they were saying.

When we got home, Chloe and I sat in the kitchen to do our math homework. Nadine sat with us at the table and opened a book. It wasn't in a language I recognized.

"What is that?" I asked.

Nadine glanced up. "I think it is Sumerian, but I am not sure."

"Uhm…what do you mean, you're not sure?"

"I do not understand all of it, but it is highly intriguing." She went back to reading like it was the most normal thing in the world for her to be reading something she didn't understand.

Chloe and I looked at each other. She shrugged and tackled her math. I looked back at Nadine and tried to figure out if she was joking. She didn't look up. I didn't think she was kidding.

I shrugged too, and opened my math book. I stared at the page for five minutes, trying to figure out if I was the one reading ancient Sumerian. I looked over at Chloe, who'd already finished with math. I let out a frustrated sigh.

"I've figured out what my kryptonite is." Chloe looked at me with a raised eyebrow. "If I'm going to be a superhero or whatever, I can save the world as long as I don't have to solve for x." Chloe rolled her eyes and looked back at her homework. Her lips curved up in the corner so I knew she was laughing at me.

"What? Go ahead and say it."

"Why don't you just close your eyes and let it come to you?" She giggled. "Miss Cleo, the fortune teller. She can't even solve a simple equation."

I made a face. "If you're so smart, why don't you help me?"

She rolled her eyes again and leaned over to look at my book. Then she burst out laughing. "You're looking at the wrong page! We're still in chapter 3, dummy!" She flipped back two chapters and pointed at some problems that were still nearly impossible.

"Oh." I blushed. "Thanks. But none of this makes any sense, either. Why does algebra have to be so hard?"

Chloe moved next to me and spent the next hour trying to explain number properties. I spent that time trying to figure out why they were even important, and wondering if Leo was thinking about me.

"If you're not going to pay attention, I'm not even going to bother," Chloe said, sitting back in her chair. She glanced at the clock. "Dad should be picking me up soon anyway. Let's watch some TV until he gets here."

I slammed my book shut. "Sounds good to me. I'm so done with math."

Chloe laughed. "Ha. Yeah, right. You would've had to do some in the first place."

I shrugged and led the way into the living room. We found a romantic comedy we'd seen a million times before, and I drifted off to sleep.

Twilight darkness surrounded me. "Is anybody there?" I recognized the voice from school, and I turned around to see her. Mrs. Britten was staring blindly around her. I waved, but she kept talking as though she didn't see me.

"I must be dreaming," she said. "Though if this is a dream, I wouldn't recognize that, would I?" She pinched her arm and cried out. "If this isn't a dream, then where in Tarnation am I? Hello? Can anybody hear me? Help!"

"I'm right here," I tried to say, but no sound came out. A movement caught my eye and I turned to see what it was. A dark shadow emerged. It was large and vaguely resembled a giraffe. I looked back at Mrs. Britten, and she was still there. Were there any other giraffes in town? *I wondered. The shadow moved closer, and I could make out a lighter shape inside the shadow. Closer, and closer still. I could almost make out a face now....*

"Tessa, wake up!" Chloe was shaking me. Hard.

"Gah! I'm up! I'm up! What are you doing?" I looked around and saw that everyone was in the living room, staring at me.

Nadine was the first one to say anything. "What is it? What did you see?"

"What do you mean? I fell asleep. I don't even have a sketch pad. I wasn't having a vision." I held up my hands to show her they were empty.

She didn't look convinced. "Fine, what was your 'dream' about?"

"Mrs. Britten was lost, I guess. It was a weird dream. I've had weird dreams before," I said uncertainly. With Nadine asking questions, I started questioning myself. It wasn't quite like the odd dreams I'd had before. Usually, those were about me walking around school naked. This one felt different, now that I thought about it.

"Better check on her, to be safe," Nadine said to my mom. Mom walked off to make a phone call. "Anything else?"

I don't know what she was expecting from me. The winning lottery numbers or something? I shook my head and got up. If I was falling asleep on the couch, I was obviously more tired than I thought. Maybe I wasn't quite recovered from all the other visions I'd had. This was getting annoying. I turned back to Nadine.

"Why am I still so tired after having

visions? I thought that forcing me to change early would help with all of this stuff."

Nadine smiled reassuringly, but not before I saw a look of concern cross her face. "I will look into it, but I am sure it is nothing."

The knock on the door let us know that Chloe's dad was here to pick her up. We said our goodbyes and she left. I slowly took the stairs up to my room. I could hear Mom and Nadine talking in the kitchen, but I couldn't hear their words. *Whatever,* I thought. *I'm tired of trying to get people to stop talking behind my back.*

I changed into a pair of blue shorts and a loose cotton shirt and crawled under my covers. I fell asleep wishing things could get back to normal.

***

When I woke up the next morning, I made the decision to make things be as close to normal as I could get them. I turned on my stereo and cranked it up while I showered. Singing along to all my favorite songs reminded me of how normal used to feel.

I cleared the steam off the mirror and danced around while I combed my hair and applied a layer of lip gloss and mascara. I went to my closet and pulled on my favorite dark blue jeans and a new purple v-neck top. I admired myself in my mirror one last time and bounced down the stairs to the kitchen. I was feeling good about myself until I saw the look on my dad's face.

I looked around. "Where's Mom? What's going on?"

Dad's lips thinned and I noticed the dark circles under his eyes. He couldn't have slept much last night. "Mom's at the clinic. Honey, sit down."

I sat and began to worry. "What's happened? Is Mom okay?"

"Mom's fine," he said quickly. He ran

his hand over his face. "It's Jane, Mrs. Britten. Mom couldn't get a hold of her last night, so she went to see her. She found her in a coma."

"Ohmygosh! What happened to her? Is she going to be okay? What-"

"There's no explanation, she's just...not waking up. Your mom's doing everything she can, but she can't sense anything wrong with her."

A million questions raced through my mind. Mom could sense illnesses, injuries – everything. If she couldn't tell what was wrong with Mrs. Britten, how would she ever be able to wake her up?

I worried all the way to Chloe's house to pick her up for school, then she worried with me when I told her what happened. When we walked into homeroom, Mrs. Mintz was sitting at the front desk. The classroom was so quiet we could probably hear a pin drop.

The bell rang and Mrs. Mintz stood up.

"Students, Mrs. Britten is not well, so I will be taking over her classes in the interim," she said, then motioned to me. "Tessa, can I speak with you in the hall, please?"

I followed her into the hall. I knew without looking that everyone was staring at me. Again. Any excitement I still had from my 'normal' routine this morning withered away.

"Tessa, have you heard anything from your mother this morning?" she asked as soon as I was through the door.

"Uhm...no," I said. Was she expecting me to know everything that was going on? Next thing, she'll be asking me if I could have a quick vision and let her know what I saw.

"Have you seen anything?" And there it was.

"I'm not a freaking fortune cookie," I muttered. Out loud, I said, "No. I haven't seen anything since yesterday. Can I go now?"

She glared at me for a second. I guess

she heard me mutter. Whatever. "Fine. Let me know if anything comes up during school."

I was already walking away so I waved back at her. I heard the anger in her voice, but I couldn't bring myself to care. I also didn't plan on reporting in every single time I had a stupid vision.

I made it back to my seat and Chloe mouthed, *"Is everything okay?"* I rolled my eyes and shook my head. I wasn't in trouble, but everything was not okay. Not that I could tell her that right then. Everyone was paying close attention to me, and all I wanted to do was sit there and, gulp, do homework.

Luckily, I didn't have time to worry about my classmates or my homework. The bell rang and I rushed off to my first advanced shifting class. I made it with plenty of time and took a seat near the back. No point in drawing any more attention to myself.

I was feeling good about getting there so

early when Tony walked in. I groaned. Fantastic, now I have classes with my older brother. I didn't know how he was going to take this, so I sat quietly and watched him.

He saw me and paused at the front of the room. Mark ran into him and looked around to see why Tony had stopped. They both stared at me for a few seconds. Then they looked at each other, had some sort of silent communication, and walked back. Tony sat next to me and Mark sat in front.

I cringed, waiting for them to start teasing me. But they surprised me.

"Dude, I'm telling you. Jacobsen is going to be the number one draft pick next year," Mark told Tony.

Tony rolled his eyes. "Yeah, right. Have you seen him run? He's going to blow his knee out before the season's over. My money's on Puller."

"You'll lose that bet, my friend," Mark

said. The bell rang and he turned to the front of the class.

Tony winked over at me before turning to the teacher, a pretty brunette with large green eyes. She looked young, probably straight out of college. She wore standard teacher clothes: a long, brown pencil skirt and a beige blouse. Someone should to tell her that she would look better in some bright colors – maybe a bright green.

I opened my notebook to sketch her in a different outfit, when I remembered that I wasn't supposed to draw until I got things under control. I sighed and closed my notebook. No point in tempting myself, and I definitely wasn't going to be taking notes, like some of the kids were doing.

She started talking about something called limited shifting and everyone opened their books. I didn't have one, so I tried to follow what she was saying. She said something about choosing what to shift, but everything she said was muffled.

I tried to focus on her words, but all I could hear was this buzzing noise. It was soft at first, but then it got louder and louder. I put my hands over my ears to try to drown it out, but it kept going.

I put my hands down and looked around. Nobody else seemed to hear it. It was just me. I felt my pencil in my hand and glanced down. Maybe....

I opened my notebook and closed my eyes.

"Oh, I hope someone can hear me!" Mrs. Britten's voice sounded like she was standing right next to me. "Please! I'm trapped. Oh, can anyone hear me?"

Darkness surrounded me, but I couldn't see anything else. What was this place, and why was Mrs. Britten here?

"Oh!" I snapped out of it so fast, I tipped over in my chair. I caught myself before I fell to the ground, but the chair clanged back onto the tile floor and everyone's eyes were on me.

"Miss Brooks, would you like to pay attention?" The teacher glared at me, her lips pursed in annoyance. What had I ever done to her? "You have made enough disturbances in other classrooms over the last week. Please do not disturb mine."

I stared at her, speechless. Of course, the only person other than me in the whole stupid town that thinks my visions are annoying, and I had her for Advanced Freak-Being. "S-sorry, Miss...uh," I paused. What was her name?

"Glenn. My name is Miss Glenn," she offered with a sneer. "You would do well to pay attention, or you will fail. This class is required for graduation from Shadow Hills High School, and I will not allow you any lenience simply because you enjoy making scenes. Is that understood?"

"Yes, Miss Glenn. It won't happen again." I slid lower in my seat and tried to hide my burning face. I blinked away the tears that threatened to fall. I'd never been called out in class, and it sucked. I looked over at Tony, and he was glaring at Miss Glenn. At least he was on my side.

The next twenty minutes were almost impossible to bear. Miss Glenn was shooting daggers every time she looked at me. I didn't have a textbook, so I couldn't hide behind that. It took all the willpower I had not to ignore what she was saying and look at my notebook. I could see a form on the page, but I couldn't make it out without concentrating. I kept glancing at it, trying to figure it out, but every time she noticed I wasn't looking at her, she raised her voice a bit.

The bell rang, and I couldn't get out of there fast enough. Tony was close behind me.

"Hey, Squirt. Don't mind her. She picks on someone every day. I should've warned you that she was a jerk." He ruffled his hand in my hair and walked off in the other direction. "Hey, Mark, wait up! Don't think I didn't see you fall asleep in class! You're lucky Dragon Lady didn't see you!"

I thought about my vision as I walked to my next class. It didn't tell me anything I didn't already know. Mrs. Britten was trapped, somehow. I didn't know where, and I didn't know how to get her out. Deciding I had nothing to report, I wouldn't go to Mrs. Mintz. There was no point, and it's not like anyone knew what'd happened.

That decided, I tried to concentrate on algebra. Tried. Why did someone think it was a good idea to put the alphabet in math? It's not like I would ever use any of this when I graduated. I don't even use this stuff in my drawing. Trying to figure out the slope of a line was pointless. If it looked right in my drawing, it was the right slope.

Speaking of drawing, I'd completely

forgotten about whatever it was that I drew last period. I turned to that page and examined it.

I sighed, disappointed. There wasn't much there. It was a lightly shaded page with a vague outline in the center. I leaned closer and tried to figure out what it was. It looked like a short cylindrical shape. Maybe a seat or something?

I blew out a breath and sat back up. I didn't have a clue what it was, which meant that it was completely worthless. Why couldn't I see what I wanted to see? The frustration of not being able to help was starting to get overwhelming.

Class let out and I wandered through the halls, wondering if I'd even go to my next class. What was the point in going? What was the point in anything? My distraction was exactly the opening that Westy needed.

"Hey there, Kitten. I knew you'd come around." He had me cornered at the end of a mostly deserted hallway. The bell rang, and everyone rushed into classrooms. We were all alone.

Chapter Fifteen

"Leave me alone, Westy. I am so not interested." I tried to get around him, but he moved to block my path. I tried again, and he crowded me against the lockers.

"You don't need to play coy with me. Not now. Nobody's watching. You're free to show your real feelings." His eyelids lowered over his pale green eyes, his mouth quirked up on one side. I'm sure he meant it to look seductive, but he just looked like he was drunk.

"My real feelings are that you're a jerk and you need to leave me alone. Now." I growled and gave him my worst glare. Chloe always laughed whenever I glared, saying I looked like I was trying hard to poop, but I hoped he got the picture.

"Aw, how sweet. I had a kitten once that made that face," he chuckled, "every time she was in the litter box."

"Go away. I mean it!" I looked around desperately, hoping one of the teachers would've noticed the noise, or the fact that students were missing from class. The halls were empty.

"I'll walk you to class when you agree to be my date for Homecoming," he said agreeably.

Wait, what? "You're nuts. I'm not going to Homecoming with you. I'm not even going at all." I didn't have a date, and the thought of asking Leo out terrified me.

"But you have to go, and I can't imagine who would look better on my arm than you." He ran his hand up and down my arm and I shuddered in revulsion. He took this as a sign of acceptance and took my hand. "We can be the most powerful couple in this school if you would stop fighting it."

Powerful? What in the world was he talking about? I knew about my power, but popularity wasn't a power. How shallow was this guy? And then it hit me – power. Mom couldn't figure out why Mrs. Britten was in a coma. Could it be that it had something to do with a shifter's power?

I searched his face for any indication that this is what he meant. All I could see was arrogance and sleaze. I took a chance. "If I was so powerful, I'd be able to help Mrs. Britten, wouldn't I?"

Something flashed across his face before disappearing behind that same mask of arrogance. I knew I had him. "Don't worry about her, Kitten. I'm sure she deserves whatever's happened to her."

Ding! Ding! Ding! An alarm went off in my head. He knew something, and I had to get it out of him. There was only one thing I could do. I almost choked on the words. "Right, fine. I'll go to Homecoming with you."

Westy grinned in triumph and stood back up, letting me free from his trap. He held out his hand and looked at me expectantly. I grasped his sweaty, clammy hand and fought a grimace. I tried desperately to smile at him, but I'm sure it looked like a cringe. I definitely had to get better at acting if I was going to get any information out of him.

He walked me to class and I ducked inside before he could lean in and kiss me. I'd already passed my gag quota for the day. I apologized to the teacher and ducked into the first seat I could find, letting out a deep breath.

I was relieved for two things. One, I was no longer in that situation, and two, I would finally find out how I could help Mrs. Britten wake up.

At lunch, I explained my theory to Chloe and Vin. They didn't seem convinced.

"I don't know, T. I mean, he's a sleaze ball, but do you really think Westy would hurt anyone?" Chloe's face was scrunched in her, "I love you, but you're being crazy" expression. It was one I knew well.

"Maybe not," I admitted. "But he knows something. He's got to. Do we know anyone else in this school that would hurt a teacher that isn't him or one of his cronies?"

Vin and Chloe sat there and thought about it. Finally, Vin spoke up. "I haven't been here long, but I think you might be right."

Chloe nodded in agreement. "Yeah, but I hope you're not."

I breathed a sigh of relief. My friends had my back again, for better or worse. "Me, too." Muscles I hadn't realized were tense loosened up. "Any suggestions on how I should get information out of him? I mean, I could try pretending that I like him, but I don't think I'm that good an actress."

Chloe snorted, and I knew we were both thinking about the time in fifth grade when I played the apple tree in our school's spring play. I'd started crying in the middle of my one line, which turned into a full-on wheezing, choking panic attack. I banned my parents from ever watching that tape, and tried to forget it ever happened.

"Maybe it won't be so bad," I tried convincing myself. "I mean, maybe I won't be quite so nervous if I'm not in front of an audience?"

My best friend raised her eyebrow, but said nothing.

I sighed. "Yeah, okay. We need to come up with a plan."

***

Apparently, we didn't need a plan. Westy met me outside after school and walked me home. He didn't notice whenever I cringed or moved away. He didn't even notice Tony glaring at him whenever he tried to grab my hand. He was so completely oblivious to everything that I was finally able to relax, knowing my plan would work. I'd get him to tell me what he knew about Mrs. Britten.

We got to my house and I ducked inside before he could even think about trying to kiss me. Even as dense as he is, he couldn't ignore vomit all over the front of his shirt.

"What was that all about, Tessa?" Tony glared and crossed his arms. His feet were planted, and I knew he wasn't going to let this slide. "Are you dating Westy?"

I sighed. I knew he wasn't going to like this, and I wasn't sure how to explain it. So, I kind of lied. "I told him what he wanted to hear so I could get to class. He cornered me in the hallway, what else was I supposed to do?"

Okay, not that big of a lie.

"You tell him 'no' and remind them that your brother will kick his sorry butt if he ever touches you again!" He threw up his hands in frustration. "Seriously, Tess! I can't believe you didn't think of that! If I'm going to be the brains *and* the brawn in this family, what are you contributing?"

I rolled my eyes, trying to figure out a way to get him off my back. "I don't need you to fight my battles, Tony. I'm going to dump him tomorrow at lunch, in front of everyone. See? Way smarter than your stupid idea."

We stared at each other for a few seconds, and I hoped he bought it. When he stopped glaring, I let out a breath. I got away with it. For today. When I didn't break up with him tomorrow, Tony would be all over me again. Maybe by then I'll either have the information I needed, or have another excuse. No way would he believe that I was dating Major Jerk face because I liked him. My stomach rolled at the thought.

"Let me know if you need help getting rid of him," Tony said. His mouth turned up in a grin. "I'd love to do some damage to that kid."

Shifting Dreams

"Right. I'll let you know." I ran up to my room and closed the door, letting out a breath. I looked around, thankful that I still had a familiar place with all of the craziness everywhere else in my life. I dropped my backpack and threw myself onto my bed.

I was so comfortable, my legs dangling over the side of the bed. My body was starting to relax from all the stress of the day when something bumped against my leg.

"Eep!" I bolted straight up, hands fisted and flailing at my unknown attacker.

"Easy! Ow! It's me!" Leo ducked behind his hands to avoid my swinging fists. I immediately stopped and stood up.

"Ohmygosh! What are you doing here?" I looked at the door, expecting Tony or someone to burst in and find out why I'd screamed. Nothing happened and I looked at Leo, who was rubbing his arm where I'd hit him and smiling shyly.

"I wanted to see you, but I didn't have your number, and I didn't think your brother would let me-" He stopped and sniffed, his eyes narrowing. "Why do you smell like another guy's sweat?"

I sniffed myself quickly, expecting to be gagged by a stench of gym socks. I didn't smell anything. "I don't...oh, Westy." I sighed. How did I explain this to Leo? It's not like we were exclusive or even dating. Technically, he didn't have the right to be jealous, but a secret part of me was kind of glad that he was.

"Are you seeing someone? Oh, jeez. I shouldn't even be here." He walked over to my window, which I hadn't noticed was open. "I'm sorry, I'll go."

"No, wait! I'm not seeing anyone! I mean, not really." I bit my lip in indecision.

Leo studied me. His eyebrow quirked and brought my attention to his eyes. I couldn't get over how amazing those eyes were. They were so distracting, I could stare at him for hours.

"Tessa? If you're not seeing someone, can you tell me why you smell like another guy?"

Dang it, I'd gotten sidetracked. "Sorry," I said. "It's kind of complicated. I promise. I'm not seeing anyone. I'm not even interested in anyone but-" *you.* I couldn't finish that sentence, but Leo grinned so I didn't think I needed to. I blushed and turned away, looking anywhere but at him. How embarrassing.

Leo sighed and ran a hand through his hair. "Look, Tessa...it's fine, okay? We're not together. I haven't even asked you out yet."

My heart fell when he said we're not together. "Wait. Yet?" I looked back at him and noticed he'd moved closer. Like, a lot closer.

"That's why I came over today. I was hoping I could take you out on Saturday?" He looked at me and I could swear he was holding his breath, waiting for my answer. Or maybe that was me.

"I'd like that," I said. A grin grew on his face and I had to dash his hopes. "But Saturday is Homecoming, and I was already asked to the dance. I'm not even interested in him, but I kind of have to go now." I looked at him apologetically. I hoped he wouldn't stop liking me. Why did I have to agree to go out with Westy? I was kicking myself right then.

"Oh," he said, looking disappointed. "What about Sunday? I mean, if you don't think you'll be too tired after the dance."

I grinned. "Absolutely. What did you have in mind?" I had a sudden panicky thought. "What about our parents? They'll never let us go out. It's not like they're the best of friends."

"Let me worry about that. So you'll go?"

I nodded, still worried. I really liked Leo, but I didn't know how my parents would react to me dating a wolf-shifter.

"Great!" Leo straightened up and I admired how tall he was. "So, can I have your number? Climbing into your bedroom window isn't as easy as it looks."

I laughed and gave him my cell phone number.

"Thanks! I'll be by at eleven. Dress comfortably!" With that, he practically leaped out the window, and I dashed over to watch him walk away. He strutted down the street, bouncing a couple of times in what looked like excitement.

I smiled and watched him until he disappeared around the corner. I couldn't believe I had a date with someone so hot. Ohmygosh. I have a date with Leo! I scrambled for my phone and called Chloe. "He asked me out!" I practically screamed when Chloe answered. "I have a date with Leo!"

The silence on the other end wasn't

exactly the response I was hoping for. "Leo, the wolf-shifter? Tessa, do you think that's a good idea?"

My excitement faded quickly. "Jeez, Chlo. I thought best friends were supposed to be excited for each other."

She sighed. "Sorry, T. I am excited for you, really. But I don't want you to get your hopes up if your parents say you can't go. We both know how they feel. Anyone who was at Tony's birthday knows how they feel."

I dropped to my bed. "I know. He's so amazing. And so hot." I bit my lip. How could I convince my parents it'd be okay? I couldn't think of anything. I sighed and I felt Chloe on the other end, commiserating with me.

"I'm sorry, T. This sucks. I may not agree with your choice of guys, but I feel for you." I heard a thump and figured she'd plopped on her bed, too. "Do you want to try meeting here? Your parents would never know."

I snorted. "Yes, they would. They know everyone in town. Someone would call them up and then I'd be in trouble for lying, too." I stared up at my ceiling and thought about it. "Honesty is the best policy, I think. Besides, maybe they'll be so impressed that I was honest that they won't mind letting me go."

This time it was Chloe who snorted. "Yeah, right. Hey, my mom's calling me. I gotta go. Good luck."

"Thanks." I hung up, feeling less excited than when I called. Until I thought about Leo, in my room, asking me out. I grinned and hugged myself. There was no way that something that felt this good was bad, right? Right. I was daydreaming when I was pulled into another vision.

"Hello?" A masculine voice called out in the darkness. A large shadow moved towards me and I stepped back, not knowing if this was friend or foe. "Hello? Is anyone out there?"

Coach Fillion stumbled in front of me, which I've never seen him do. He was a large man, but oddly, the word 'graceful' fit him well.

"Who's there?" A woman's voice cried out. Mrs. Britten stumbled around and crashed into Coach. "Oh!"

"Jane? Jane! I'm so glad I found you! Where have you been?" Coach grabbed Mrs. Britten's shoulders and looked her over, like he was checking for injuries.

"Right here, Malcolm. I've been right here all this time. I don't know where we are, but I can't find a way out." Mrs. Britten sobbed and Coach comforted her, looking around.

"We'll figure it out, Jane. Someone will find us. I'm sure of it." He looked directly at me and our gazes locked. I didn't think he could see me, but he could definitely sense I was there. "Help us."

"Owww!" I sat straight up in bed and immediately fell back when my brain tried to escape from behind my eyeballs. Ohmygosh, that hurt!

I curled up in bed, massaging my temples. What the heck did I just see? What do these visions mean? How was I supposed to help anyone if I couldn't even sit up after seeing these things? I had to talk to Nadine, pronto.

Struggling to stand up, I stumbled my way down the stairs. I was making a lot of noise, so I wasn't surprised when Mom and Nadine came out of the kitchen. Mom ran up and helped me down the rest of the stairs while Nadine rushed to her room, probably for some more of those nasty energy things. At least, I hoped that's what she was getting.

"What did you see, honey?" Mom brushed my hair off the side of my face and checked my eyes, looking for a concussion or something. It felt good to have her taking care of me, but I needed some answers before I was going to give any.

Nadine came back with an armful of snacks, and I wondered why she had so many. It was almost like she expected this to happen.

"Why am I so weak and in so much pain when I have these episodes?" I asked, gulping a chalky drink that I think was supposed to be chocolate-flavored. "And why aren't you more surprised that it's happening?"

I stared at her, trying to give her the evil eye, but probably only ended up looking constipated. Mom seemed surprised, whether it was because I didn't answer her or because of the question I asked, I don't know. She glanced back and forth between Nadine and me, deciding if she should interfere. I reached over and squeezed her hand. I didn't need her help in this one.

Nadine was shell-shocked for a couple of seconds before she sighed and slumped to the chair across from us. "You are right. I expected something like this to happen." She held up her hands when I glared harder. "I did not know exactly what might happen, but I prepared for several possibilities."

"Why?" It was a simple question, but my life seemed to depend on the answer.

"You came into your power so young, there is not much precedent. There are not many accounts in the archives about this kind of thing, but the ones that are there are bad." She paused, her gaze ping-ponging between Mom and me, like she deciding something. She took a small breath and went on. "You have heard of Pompeii, right? Learned all about it in school, maybe the History Channel or something?"

Mom and I both nodded and she continued. "That was the result of someone who came into his powers way too young. He was fourteen, and nobody was prepared for what he could do. He had no control over his emotions or powers and they all combined into a massive, destructive force."

She let this sink in for several moments.

"I think the reason you are experiencing the pain and weakness is because you have not fully accepted your new place in society."

I looked up at her sharply. What was she talking about? I didn't have a place in society other than being me. Same old Tessa Jean Brooks that I've always been. Just because I sometimes walked on four paws and ate kibble didn't change that. Did it?

"Do not look at me like that, little one. You have not fully dealt with your new situation. I hate to be the one to tell you, and I am sure your parents do not want to acknowledge it either, but you have a massive responsibility. You can see things that can save lives. You can see the future, the present, and probably even the past if you tried hard enough. That makes you an asset to so many people – including those who may want to use you for terrible things.

"Your power is so strong that your body could not wait until your seventeenth birthday to release it. I do not know anyone born in at least four decades who have had even close to that much power."

Scowling at her, I decided this had to be a joke. I couldn't possibly be the most powerful shifter in forty years. I was only...me.

I was still glaring at her when she said, "You need to find the balance between both aspects of yourself, or your headaches and blackouts and weakness will only continue to worsen."

"What do you mean, find the balance? You just told me I'm some all-powerful Chosen One, and then you give me the stupid advice to 'find the balance?' Are you freaking crazy?" I was getting mad. This chick didn't even know me, and now she was flipping my world upside down and all she could say was 'find the balance?'

I stood up. I was still dizzy, and my head felt like a cannonball, but no way was I going to sit here and let this stranger tell me that I had no choice but to be some magical eight-ball for the shifter community. "If you figure out you have any more genius advice for me, I'll be in my room." I realized I hadn't mentioned my vision. I turned to Mom. "Check on Coach Fillion. I think he might be hurt."

Forcing myself not to wobble, I walked up the stairs. I shut the door and leaned back heavily. My knees were shaking from exhaustion and all I could think about was passing out. I threw myself halfway across the room and landed in the middle of my bed, face down.

When I closed my eyes, a vortex of color greeted me. The tunnel of light and shadow I saw when I was this tired was usually familiarly comforting, but now it reminded me of all the terrible things I'd seen lately. I groaned and opened my eyes. The last thing I needed was to keep stressing on these stupid visions that made absolutely no sense to me.

Shifting Dreams

Flopping to my back, I stared at the ceiling. There was no way I would be able to sleep without seeing people wandering around in darkness, lost and scared. I blew out a breath. Now that I was alone with my thoughts, I was bored. I could do my homework. No, thanks. Read for fun? I didn't have any new books lying around.

Not being allowed to draw made life so much more difficult, and way less fun. I was always drawing whenever I had free time, so now I had no idea what to do. There was never anything good on TV, so I rarely bothered flipping the channels since it was such a waste of time. But time was something I had a lot of right now.

Having nothing better to do, I flopped back in bed and turned on my flat screen. I got it last year for Christmas. Mom had a little shopping problem that came in handy around Black Friday. I convinced her it was a good deal, and I promised to act surprised whenever I opened the box. It was a win-win situation for all of us. Except for Dad, I guess. He's the one who paid that bill.

I flipped through channels and wondered who would actually watch some of these shows. I ran across one of those reality singing shows and turned it up. These stupid shows were my guilty pleasure. I especially loved the first few episodes of the season. Watching some of those auditions made me feel better about my complete inability to sing. I settled in for the hour, wishing I had popcorn or something that I could munch on. Oh, well. I wasn't about to leave my room for anything short of a house fire.

My cell phone buzzed and I picked it up.

Hi.

That's all it said. I didn't recognize the number at all. When I first got my phone, I sent more than ten messages to the wrong number before they told me I'd made a mistake. I was nicer than that person, so I wrote:

Sry, wrong nmbr.

I put my phone down and turned the TV up even more. This looked like it was going to be a good audition. And by good, I mean bad. Before the lady with the bad extensions and purple and silver polka-dotted dress could sing, my phone buzzed again. I groaned in frustration and picked it up.

But this is the number you gave me.

Weird. My TV was making a dog-awful noise and I looked up with a grin. Score! Bad hair lady was definitely worse than me. I tuned out the judges, who were telling her she should have a surgeon remove her vocal cords and glanced back at the phone.

I dont kno this nmbr

I was at the end of my patience for wrong number person. And the next audition had a great back story, which meant he was going to get through. I knew I had to sit through the good singers to get to the bad ones, but dang it, why did they have to be so good? My phone buzzed again. I was going to ignore it, but I decided I'd send one last message and tell them to leave me alone.

Tessa. Is this you? It's Leo.

Gah! I couldn't believe I didn't think of that. I felt my cheeks warm, and I was glad he wasn't there to see.

Sry Leo. Didnt know ur nmbr. Sup?

I didn't put my phone down this time. I barely glanced up when the next audition came up. Another good one. I turned the TV down and stared at my phone. It buzzed.

Just thinking about you. Couldn't wait until Sunday to talk to you.

I couldn't breathe. This hottie couldn't stop thinking about me? Okay, that's not what he said, but I'm sure that's what he meant. I did a tiny happy dance in my bed and forced myself to say something cool back.

Thinking abt u 2.

Okay, not exactly the most intelligent or witty response.

What are you up to? I spent 30 minutes trying to read before texting you.

Wow, he actually couldn't stop thinking about me. I couldn't stop grinning. I was hooked.

Jst watching TV. Head hrts from visions.

I glanced back up in time to see a man wearing a tutu walk out of the audition room. Dang it, I missed an awesomely bad one! I wasn't too sad, considering why I'd missed it. My phone buzzed again.

Sorry. Can't they fix it? I don't know much about other traits, but I didn't think they should hurt you.

I snorted, thinking about Nadine's solution.

They expect me 2 fix it. Smthing abt

accepting myself. Rly helpful. :-(

I sighed over the problem. I'd gone out of my way to 'see' things and changed loads of times, so I wasn't sure how much more 'accepting' I could be of the situation.

Oh, I had that problem, but it didn't hurt me. I just had trouble changing sometimes.

How was that the same problem? I didn't get a chance to ask, because my phone buzzed again.

I meditated and sort of 'met' the wolf inside me. It was weird, but I haven't had problems since.

I looked at my phone in confusion. He met the wolf? Like it's a separate part of him or something? I thought about it for a few minutes. I mean, I guess it made sense, kind of like two sides of the same coin.

Thnx. Ill try it. Cant hrt rite?

I turned my TV off and moved to the

floor. I didn't know much about meditating but, in all the movies, they sat cross-legged on the floor. I cracked my neck and shook my arms and head to loosen up. My phone buzzed and I grabbed it quickly, smacking my hand against my bed frame. I shook it, trying to make the pain go away and read the message.

Nope. Let me know how it goes. I'll be thinking of you.

Now I was thinking about him. I needed to clear my mind, because that's what they always did in the movies. I had no idea if I was doing this right, but I would find out soon enough.

My hand throbbed, but it wasn't too distracting. I leaned back against my bed and closed my eyes. I breathed in deeply and slowly exhaled. My finger twitched. I imagined sitting in an empty room. White walls, white floor, white ceiling. I focused on my breathing. In. Out. In. Out.

Nothing happened. I blew out a breath of frustration and opened my eyes. Except I didn't see my room. I saw the white room. Wow. I looked around and found myself standing without actually moving a muscle. "Hello?" I said. My voice sounded flat and wrong in this space.

You've finally come to greet me, Dream Walker.

I whipped around and jumped away from the giant panther standing directly in front of me. Was it talking to me?

I speak into your mind. You may do the same. You have questions. Ask.

Her voice was smooth and dark. It made my bones vibrate and gave me goose bumps on top of goose bumps. I shook off my anxiety and concentrated on what was happening. *WHY IS THIS HAPPENING TO ME?*

The cat leaned back, cringing. I guess I didn't need to concentrate that hard. *You are strong. Embrace your strength, and accept mine. Together, we will be complete. You will be limitless.*

What did that mean? *You make it sound so easy. How do I do all of this? What do you mean limitless? Everything has limits.*

She cocked her head to the side and I swear she smiled. *You do not have limits, Dream Walker. You can control the world, if you so wish. The power I give you only needs to be honed and you can know everything there is, in this world and the next.*

I moved back. *I don't want to rule the world. I want to be me. And why do you keep calling me Dream Walker?*

Because that is who you are. You walk through dreams, those of the past, present, and future. The extent of your powers is only limited by you. She lifted a paw. *It is all up to you now. I have told you all I can. Embrace me now and discover your strength.*

She stared at me, her tail twitching back and forth, her paw hovering in front of her. Was I ready for this? I didn't want to have the powers she offered, but it didn't seem like I had a choice. *If I touch you, it'll stop hurting every time I have a vision?*

Her head went down in a small nod. I braced myself and reached out to her. My fingers sunk into her soft fur, and I felt my body change. I was panther, I was human. We were one.

There was no going back now.

Chapter Sixteen

I was back in my body, sitting in my bedroom. I opened my eyes to see the familiar sights. My things were all there, but everything was altered somehow. It wasn't that anything was different, but I knew that everything had changed.

Moving around, I stretched. Nothing hurt anymore, but a spot on my right side felt tight, like the skin was dry or something. I lifted my shirt and stared at the mirror, stunned at what I saw. A scar, fully healed like I'd had it for years. It looked like I'd been attacked by a leopard, and I suppose that I had. The four uneven lines told me a story about who I was, and who I could become. I'd been marked.

I knew that I'd given her permission

when I touched her, just like I knew I needed to keep this a secret. I couldn't show anyone, though I couldn't say why. I pulled my shirt back over the scar. My heart pounded, and I felt a desperate need to talk to someone. I couldn't talk to Chloe. She wouldn't understand. Leo was...I wanted to trust him, and I felt like I could, but the thought of talking to him didn't feel quite right. My inner child was screaming for my Mommy, and I couldn't resist the cry.

Running out the door, I went down the stairs into the kitchen where I ran straight into her arms. I sobbed. She comforted me. She sang a soft song I remembered from when I was younger. I held on even after I had no more tears.

"You are so strong, honey." Mom brushed my hair back. "You'll get through this. I'm so proud of you."

She didn't say any more, but it wasn't necessary. We'd always understood each other. I felt better than I had in weeks, so I helped her finish making dinner. When Dad got home,

Mom gave him a look and he somehow understood. He hugged me and went upstairs to change. Dinner was quiet, with only the sounds of clinking silverware and Tony burping and shoveling his way through the food.

Nadine came back later, when I was in my room. She'd missed dinner, but I'm sure that was on purpose. She knocked softly, but didn't wait for me to answer before she walked in. Her eyes scanned me from head to toe, and I shifted uncomfortably. She gently settled herself into my desk chair. For someone whose other half was so large and clumsy, she moved very gracefully. "So it is done, then. How do you feel?"

"I feel fine. I'm not in pain anymore." I paused, my eyebrows coming together in confusion and anger. "Why didn't you tell me it was so easy? Why didn't you tell me how it was done? Why did you make me go through all of that in the first place and make me guess how to make it better?"

She sighed and looked at her hands.

When her gaze met mine, her mouth quirked to the side and she looked kind of guilty. "I did not know what was necessary. Obviously, I have read about shifters who had to commune with their other half, but I never experienced that myself. Not many have the need to do anything other than shift on their birthday to experience the full range of their abilities. There is no indication of how to commune in any of the texts I have read. It seems to be a big secret amongst those who have done it."

Nadine's big brown eyes searched my face, and I got the feeling she was trying to ask me to tell her what I'd done without actually asking. If it was some big secret, I wasn't going to be the one who let the proverbial cat out of the bag. I shrugged.

Her face fell in disappointment. "Yes, well. It is done, and you are obviously better for it. This is for the best anyway." She picked at some invisible lint on her pants. "I need to return to the Library soon. My leave is almost over."

She seemed disappointed, but also

excited to be going back to work. "What do you do there, anyway?" I was curious. She'd never talked about her job, or her life. I didn't know anything about her.

She glanced up, smiling. "I read. It is wonderful, actually. I read and translate texts so others may understand. I organize the information so others may find the information they need without searching terribly long." She paused, and lowered her voice conspiratorially, leaning closer. "When I got there, they had scrolls from the Byzantine right next to scrolls from the English Renaissance! And they were not even about the same topics!" With a gasp, she leaned back.

She clearly expected me to be appalled, so I tried my best. "That's uhm...awful." I never said my best was very good. But she didn't seem to notice.

She lifted her eyebrows. "And that is not even the worst part! They had Latin texts right next to Olde English texts and Atlantian texts!"

"Wow," I said, widening my eyes in

fake shock. Wait, what? "Atlantian texts? Are you telling me that Atlantis was real?"

"Oh," she said, chewing her lower lip. "Forget I said that, okay? I could get into so much trouble!"

She stared at me with worry until I mimed zipping my lips and throwing away the key.

"Great!" She stood up. "I will return to my room now, unless there is anything else you wished to discuss?"

"Nope. I'm good. See ya." I was still reeling from the news that Atlantis really existed, and I wanted to do some research to see what I could find. I knew it some mythical place that disappeared, but I didn't know much else about it.

I researched for a while, coming up with loads of theories, but none of them fit together. In one place, Atlantis was supposed to be some super advanced civilization, in another it was no more advanced than ancient Egypt. Some said it was in the Mediterranean, others said it was in the middle of the Atlantic.

I yawned. It was getting late. I wasn't going to solve that ancient mystery tonight, so I changed into pajamas and crawled into bed. I was asleep almost as soon as my head hit the pillow.

Mrs. Britten and Coach Fillion were sitting back to back, staring off into space. Occasionally, she would sigh and he would respond with a grunt. They looked so sad and pathetic I wished I could do something to help them.

"Hey! Can anyone hear me?" A guy's voice called out. "Hello? This is so not cool, guys! Where am I?"

As one, the three of us turned toward the voice. It sounded terrifyingly familiar, and I hoped I was wrong.

Tony appeared from the shadows, stumbling backwards, searching for his bearings. "Hey! Come on, let me out!"

"Brooks! Over here," Coach called out, standing up. He and Tony met in the middle,

where Coach checked him for injuries.

"Coach? What are you doing here?" Tony scanned the area. "Where is here?"

The man's mouth flattened into a grim line. "I'm not sure, Brooks, but we'll get out of here. We'd about given up hope, but I guess we can't do that now that you're here."

Mrs. Britten joined them, rubbing her arms like she was cold. "I'm not sure that we can get out of here by ourselves, Malcolm."

Coach didn't say anything, but he nodded slightly in agreement. "We can't give up now. We can't let this go on any longer."

Again, he looked straight at me, like he was seeing me. "Someone needs to come in after us. I think it's the only way."

The people faded into darkness and I was alone. "How do I help them? What good are all of my powers if I can't save my own brother?"

I searched, desperate to find something. I don't know what I was expecting. My panther, maybe? Nothing appeared, and I felt defeated.

Shifting Dreams

Suddenly, images began to flash around me. My face, eyes closed in sleep. A crystal pedestal. Hands clasped together. A flash of metal flying through the air. A forest shrouded in darkness.

The images surrounded me, closing in. I couldn't breathe! I knew I had to wake up and I-

Sitting up, I gasped for air. I ran to my bathroom and splashed cold water on my face. I stared into the mirror, my expression wild. My lips trembled and my cheeks were flushed. I took a deep breath and let it out slowly. And I understood what I had to do.

I realized something else in that instant, too. "Ohmygosh!" I stumbled out of my bedroom and ran across the hall to Tony's room. He was there, sleeping peacefully. Drool dripped out of his mouth onto his pillow.

"Tony?" I approached, hoping that he would wake up any second and throw me out of his room. He didn't move. I pushed the bed with my foot, shaking him a little. "Tony? Wake up!"

No movement. I stood over him and

shook his shoulder, hard. "Tony, wake up!" He didn't move, except to continue to breathe. My dream wasn't a prophecy, it had already happened. I ran into the hallway and pounded through my parents' door. Their bed was made and the room was empty. I ran down the stairs into the kitchen, where Dad was eating breakfast and Mom was drinking coffee.

"Mom, come quick! It's Tony!" I didn't wait for her to respond, running back up the stairs and into his room. I turned on the light and opened his curtains, hoping I was wrong, that the sudden light would make him chase me and give me a noogie. I turned around to look. He was still lying in bed.

Mom rushed in and looked at him. She started with his head, searching intently as she worked her way down. When she carefully peeled his covers back, I turned away. She let out a sob and I rushed over to her.

On the front of his hip, just above his pants line, there was a small mark. Three ovals stacked on top of each other, with the smallest on the bottom and the biggest at the top.

I glanced up at her, confused. "What's that, Mom? What does it mean?"

She shook her head, still clearly upset. "I don't know. But I found the same mark on the other two patients. Your teachers both have it, one on the back of the neck, one on the shoulder." She took a deep breath to calm down. I don't think it worked. "I can't find anything wrong with them, and I haven't found anything that will wake them up!"

She sat on the bed and stroked Tony's hair back. I know she was hoping it would be enough to wake him up. It used to work for us all the time. It didn't do anything this time.

I remembered the epiphany I'd had this morning, before I'd run to Tony's room. "Mom, I think I know what to do."

Standing abruptly, she turned to me, hope reflected in her eyes. "What? Why didn't you tell me before? Let's go!"

I shook my head, upset that I had to tell her no. "We can't do it right now. It has to be done between sunset and sunrise in order to work."

It seemed like she was going to say something else. Maybe something along the lines of, 'Young lady, you do what you're told,' but she took a deep breath shook her head. "Okay, what do you need me to do?"

I thought about it for a second, to recall exactly what I'd seen in my vision. "I need Tony and the other two, together. We all need to be in that cave where I changed."

It was actually the only thing I was sure about the vision. I remembered the flashes in my dream, and I still didn't know what they all meant. But there was no point in telling my mom this. She was worried enough as it was.

She was nodding, already standing up and putting away her medical things. "Okay, is there anything else?"

"No, Mom," I went over and hugged her. "It'll be okay," I whispered. I hoped I was right.

***

I went through the rest of the morning in a haze. I went to school like it was a normal day in the life of me. For all I knew, maybe this is what my life had become. I was in the middle of wallowing in despair when Chloe snapped her fingers in front of my eyes.

"Tessa! Snap out of it!" I looked at her. She looked agitated, which meant she'd been probably trying to talk to me for a while. "What is with you today? You're acting like a zombie, and it's not like you."

I shook my head and smiled weakly. "Sorry, Chlo, distracted, I guess."

I wasn't sure why I didn't want to tell Chloe about what had happened yesterday. The whole thing with meeting my panther in my head was weird. I mean, the panther is me, and I am the panther, right? So basically I'd had some weird conversation with...myself? And that made my dreams and weird second sight somehow align with...what?

If I was being honest with myself, the whole thing still had me reeling. I didn't understand it enough to explain it to Chloe, and I knew that she definitely wouldn't understand. She'd try, but there was no way she could, without going through the same thing herself. So, I kept quiet.

The fact that Tony was in a coma had spread through the school like wildfire. Chloe had jumped all over me when I'd told her this morning, but I didn't want any more sympathy. I had a plan to help everyone. I just didn't want it to spread through the school that I was going to be the one that cured everyone. What if I couldn't do it? I wasn't sure I was interpreting the vision correctly. What if I messed up and made it worse? I could lose Tony, Coach, *and* Mrs. Britten forever.

Just thinking about tonight made me feel sick to my stomach and my upper lip sweat. I was scared about what I was going to do, but I didn't want Chloe or anyone else catching on to that. Especially my mom. If word got to her that I was anxious about anything, she wouldn't let me do it. I'd let people keep thinking I was worried about Tony.

Chloe's eyebrows furrowed in concern and she bit her lip. "Is there anything I can do for you? Ice cream and Evan Balney night?" Evan Balney was our favorite half-naked TV hunk.

I shook my head. Tonight was definitely not the night for movies and junk food. I had to start the ritual as soon as the sun went down, because I didn't know how long it was all going to take. "Thanks, Chloe. I'll take you up on that one after everyone wakes up, I think."

She continued to watch me with a worried frown, but I shrugged it off. There was nothing she could do, for me or anyone else.

I didn't learn anything all day. I sat in my classes and wandered the halls and thought about nothing but what I'd be doing that night. I closed my eyes and tried to contact that other place, where Tony was lost. I wanted to somehow let him know I was coming. But I never saw anything but the normal eyes-closed shadows.

When I got home that afternoon, I ignored my homework and collected food from the kitchen. I didn't know if I'd need more energy than normal for what I was about to do. Sure, I'd connected with myself yesterday, but that didn't necessarily mean I no longer needed the calories. I ate a few cookies and nervously waited for Dad to get home.

Mom was setting the cave up and Dad was going to bring me over so we could start as soon as the sun set. Mom wanted to keep an eye on everyone's vital signs to make sure nobody was in danger. It was an experiment for everyone, and she wanted it to be as safe as possible. I hoped she wouldn't make me stop when she saw the way my heart was beating.

Dad got home, looking calm but sweaty. He always got really calm whenever he was the most anxious or scared. This put me even more on edge, but I tried not to show it.

We arrived at the clearing and got out of the car to walk the rest of the way. When we reached the cave, I paused, breathing deeply. "I can do this," I whispered under my breath. I left my shoes at the cave entrance and walked in.

Three gurneys stood around the crystal pedestal, each holding someone hooked up to a saline solution. I tried to see Tony, but couldn't. The cave was almost as full of people as when I'd been there last. Everyone whispered to each other, stopping one by one to stare at me.

I found Mom in the crowd and raised my eyebrows in a question. She shrugged sympathetically and came over to squeeze my shoulders. "They're here to give you support," she said. She examined the group and lowered her voice. "They want to make sure nobody gets hurt."

"Oh, great. So no expectations at all, right?" There wasn't enough air there. I retraced my steps and left the cave. I glanced at the sun and decided I had a few minutes.

I barely even had the thought before I'd changed and was running toward the trees. I climbed up and stretched out across a thick branch, going over my plan again in my head. A few minutes passed and I heard my Dad walk out.

"It's time," he called softly, and went back inside.

I released a panther sigh and jumped back to earth, changing back in mid-stride. I'd never felt more comfortable in my own skin. Feeling better about myself than I had in weeks, Mom hooked me up to wires and a beeping machine. I lay down on a mat next to the center pedestal.

I felt the sun go down and closed my eyes. *Game time.*

Chapter Seventeen

I opened my eyes and scanned the area around me. The surroundings were familiar. I congratulated myself on being able to get there on purpose. I hoped it would set a new pattern for me, only seeing what I want to see, and not having these things shoved on me when I was in the middle of a sentence. I could only imagine what would happen once I started driving. I shuddered and pushed the thought away.

Focus, Tessa, *I told myself.*

I studied the area around me, wondering where I should go. My gut told me to start walking, so I did. It's not like this place had any landmarks or distinctive features. Just bland and dark and slightly foggy.

A noise sounded nearby, but I couldn't

place it. I paused to listen. I heard it again to my left, so I changed direction. I walked carefully, not sure what I would find. A dark figure up ahead scared me into a cautious crouch. I couldn't tell if it was friend or foe, so I snuck up slowly. It didn't take me long to recognize Tony's signature messy 'do, so I rushed over to him.

He was sitting, slouched over himself.
Am I too late?

I noticed that even here, wherever this was, I needed to breathe. I checked Tony and felt relief when I saw his chest rise and fall. I shook him, but true to form, he was impossible to wake up. I wished I had a glass of water or something to throw on him, but I'd have to figure out another way to get him out.

I looked around for Mrs. Britten and Coach. I saw a large lump of person not far from Tony. I didn't want to leave him, but I figured I wasn't going far. I walked to the lump and saw that the other two were sitting back to back, slumped over their legs. My attempt at waking them up didn't work any better than with Tony. What was wrong with them?

I looked back and forth between the three of them, occasionally pushing at the adults with my foot, hoping they'd snap out of it. I was about to try lifting Mrs. Britten, the only one I could conceivably carry when I was scared out of my shorts.

"Nice of you to drop by," a voice boomed. I turned to see a big man emerge from the shadows.

"Who are you, and what have you done with them?" My voice didn't tremble, but my hands sure did. I needed to know who this was and if I had any chance of getting rid of him before he turned me into kitty stew. What I saw made me gasp.

The creature stood on two thickly muscled legs, covered in brown fur. He wore no shoes – probably because his feet featured razor-sharp claws at the end of each toe. His torso was ripped and hairy too, black with grey stripes going up to his shoulders. His arms were long and athletic. Long fingers uncurled to reveal thin, pointed talons at the end of each finger. His neck was long, thick, and spotted. His face was indescribable. It kept changing, melding into some horrifying impression of life. A snout, no, a beak, no, a human nose – there was no constant. Except the eyes. The eyes were black and completely terrifying.

I took a step back and the thing laughed, a deeply disturbing sound. It enjoyed my fear, flexing its muscles and shaking its monstrous head.

"P-please," I stammered. "Let them go." I didn't think it would listen, but I had to try. I had no idea how I could possibly save them if this beast didn't cooperate.

The monster laughed again. "Run home, little kitty. Run away, before I decide to keep you as trophy number four!" He held up four taloned fingers before swiping at me. I was barely fast enough to jump out of the way.

I searched for anything that could help me. All I saw were the limp bodies of my brother and teachers. I was on my own with no weapons, no chance.

I stared the monster down, determined. "Fine. I'm leaving. But if anything happens to any of these people, you'll pay."

It laughed again, taking a step toward me. "Don't threaten me, little one. You don't know who you're dealing with." It swiped at me again, but I wasn't fast enough this time and one of its talons caught my arm.

Searing pain brought me out of my daze, screaming. I cut off the sound abruptly. Mom rushed to my side to check on me. I dared a glance at my arm and saw blood everywhere. Apparently that old myth was true. Whatever injuries you suffer in a dream state show up in the real world. Well, that was fantastic. And all for nothing, too.

My brother lay in his hospital bed, an IV in his arm. He looked so fragile. I never thought I'd use that word to describe him. It kind of depressed me to see my big bear of a brother that way. My arm stung but I couldn't waste time worrying about that.

What went wrong? I could've sworn all I needed to do was enter the weird dream world, pull them out, be a hero. I thought about my epiphany dream. Cave – check. Forest – that had to be the forest outside – check. Hands clasped together – well, I'd done that. What about the flash of metal? I focused on that part of the vision but was unable to determine what the metal was, or its significance to the ritual.

I sighed in frustration as Mom hovered over me, examining my arm. She'd been quiet, letting me think. But her nervous energy forced me back into the present. She needed an explanation, and so did the rest of the adults watching me.

"I'm sorry, I must've missed something." I shook my head. "I couldn't save them. There was this thing there. I think it was waiting for me."

I looked down, embarrassed that I'd even thought I could do anything to help. I was a kid. I wasn't anyone who could help. I should leave the important stuff to the adults. At least they knew what they were doing.

"What do you mean, honey? There was someone else there?" Mom gently touched my arm. "Is that how you got this cut?"

I glanced at the gash. "Yeah. There was some kind of monster. Big, scary, mean." I looked around, self-conscious about everyone staring at me. I'd described the boogey man, and most of them appeared disappointed and annoyed. A couple of them started talking, and my cheeks flushed. I was just another kid, afraid of the dark.

"Honey, I'm proud of you." Mom touched my chin and forced me to look at her. "You were so brave tonight."

"Brave," I snorted. "Right. So brave, I woke up screaming. So brave, I couldn't even save one person from that *thing*. I knew I wasn't anything special, and this proves it. Can I go home now?"

"Okay, sweetheart. I'd like you to shift sometime tonight so you can heal that arm, but otherwise, you seem to be fine."

I hugged Mom and stood up from the mat to hug Dad. My head felt light for a second, but I didn't stop. I didn't want Mom to keep me there any longer. I was fine, but I had to get out of this cave. It felt suddenly small and cramped, with eyes staring at me, judging me.

I didn't want to wait for Dad, so I walked out of the cave and grabbed my shoes on the way. Pine needles littered the ground and poked into my feet, but I quickly got used to it. I heard Dad running behind me, and he caught up with me, gasping for breath.

"Where did you learn that?"

I didn't know what to say. I mean, all I did was go to sleep or into a trance or whatever. I looked at him, prepared to shrug his question off, but he wasn't looking at me. Not my face, anyway. He was staring at my feet. I looked down and jumped, startled.

My feet were furry and black. They were panther feet. I hadn't gotten used to the pine needles. My feet had changed to become more resistant to the prickly leaves. "Ohmygosh! How did that happen and how can I change it back?" My voice sounded whiny, even to me. I didn't care at all – I wanted it fixed!

"Calm down, sweetheart. It's fine. Lots of shifters can shift parts of themselves without shifting their whole bodies." Dad's hand on my shoulder forced me to focus on breathing to calm myself. His mouth turned down into a puzzled frown. "Usually they have to concentrate on it, though."

He stared at me for a second. I'm sure he was wondering why he had to be the one with the monster for a daughter. Then he smiled and kissed my forehead. "Calm down and envision your feet changing. It's not much different from a normal whole-body change."

He stepped back. I wasn't sure what he thought about this new development, but he seemed to be acting normal. He wasn't totally freaking out on me, so it must not have been too weird.

I closed my eyes and imagined my feet

and I suddenly felt the prickly pine needles poking in between my toes. I smiled and looked at the ground, glad to see my feet again. Then I frowned and saw I desperately needed a pedicure. I hadn't done my nails since before all this craziness happened and they looked sad. I quickly put on my shoes and walked with Dad to the car.

We were both quiet for a while, but then I couldn't stand it anymore. "So can you do it?"

Dad glanced over at me and quickly back at the winding road. He didn't pretend to not know what I was talking about. "No, I can't," he said quietly. "There are a few people in town who can, but it's not a very common ability. When I was in school they taught us about it. We all tried to shift our hands or feet, but few of us could do it."

He chuckled, remembering something. "One boy in my class, Marty, was able to grow his tail. It took him three days of trying to fully shift and then shift back to get rid of it. Everyone called him Monkey Marty for the rest of school." He looked thoughtful. "He's a senator now."

I grinned, imagining how funny it would be to grow a tail. Then I thought about what he'd said. "Wait, it took him three days to shift? Why couldn't he just close his eyes and shift like me?" How weird was I?

Dad glanced over again, and took a second to answer. "We all have different levels of ability, both with our traits and our shifting. I never had problems shifting all the way, even when I first turned seventeen. Your mom had more difficulty, but she practiced a lot and was able to do it easily enough within a month or so.

"Some adults still have to concentrate hard to achieve their shift. They usually prefer to live away from the big Shifter communities like Shadow Hills. Many own or rent cabins away from civilization so they can go there to unwind in their animal forms for a week or so every couple of months. It's easier for them that way."

I nodded. It made sense that there were different levels of shifting ability. Like some people are good at math and others are good at art. Maybe I was just a super-genius in the art of Shifting. This made me feel a little better.

The silence continued in the car, but it wasn't uncomfortable. Of course, that may be because I fell asleep halfway home. I was exhausted, and it was late. Dad woke me up when we arrived, and I was awake only long enough to change into pj's and fall into bed. I didn't even bother crawling under the covers. It was a blessedly dreamless sleep.

***

The next day was Saturday. Usually, Mom was up and outside, pulling weeds or watering her pansies. But Tony was in the hospital, which meant Mom was there, too. I knew she was working her hardest to find a way to wake everyone up. She'd been frustrated for days, because her medivoyance wasn't helping at all. She'd tried all the latest medical tests, and even modern science was failing.

I rubbed my eyes and walked downstairs to get breakfast. I was still upset about my failure yesterday, and I needed sustenance so I could determine what went wrong.

Nadine was already in the kitchen, reading one of her gibberish books. She glanced up quickly, but then did a double-take. "What happened to you?" She sounded horrified, and I wondered how bad I looked. I hadn't even glanced at myself since yesterday, and I could only imagine what she saw. I wondered briefly whether I cared, and decided I didn't.

"Rough night. I tried waking everyone up, but it didn't go like I planned." My voice sounded so scratchy and dejected, it depressed me even more. I reached for a bowl from the cupboard.

Suddenly, Nadine was all up in my face. "What do you mean? What did you try?"

"Ow!" I yelled when she grabbed my injured arm. I remembered that I could shift and heal the injury. I backed away from her to change, then quickly shifted back, glancing at my arm. The ache was still there, so I removed the bandages. I squinted at the wound the creature had scored into my skin, the wound that was still there despite my shift. "How did that not heal?"

"Where did you get that injury?" Nadine scowled. "Was it when you attempted to rescue the others?"

"Yeah, but it didn't work." I grimaced, moving my arm. It wasn't bleeding anymore, so I didn't bother to put the bandages back on. "I tried dreaming about waking them up, but this is the only thing that happened."

"Why would you think you could do that? Only Dream Walkers can affect dreams and, wait, are you a Dream Walker? That is *fantastic*!" Nadine grinned excitedly. The scowl on my face must have let her know she was acting like a lunatic. Her grin disappeared. "Of course, your injury is not fantastic. There is nothing to be done about that, I am afraid. Injuries received during Dream Walking can only be healed by time."

Great. Exactly what I wanted to hear. I almost jumped out of my skin when Nadine let out a yelp.

"Oh, my! I know exactly what to do now!" She stared into space for a minute, like she was scanning some obscure text only she could see. "Yes! That is the one!" She grinned at me. "Okay, are you ready for this?"

She didn't wait for a nod or anything, just spouted off some gibberish. I had no idea what she said, but she sure seemed excited about it. I watched her dumbly, waiting for her to notice me. When she finally did, she cocked her head curiously. "Why are you not excited? We solved the problem!"

Sure we did. "What are you talking about? I have no idea what you said. How is that supposed to solve the problem?"

Her mouth popped open like she was going to say something, and then she quickly closed it. Then her eyebrows rose to her hairline and she jumped out of her seat. She rushed to the guest room, where she'd been staying since her arrival, and ran back, scribbling on a notepad. She shoved the paper in my hands and I scrambled to take it. What I held in my hand might have vaguely resembled writing, but not in any language I recognized. I sighed and handed it back to her. "What am I supposed to be seeing?"

She glanced at the page and huffed. "Rats! Hold on, I will get it this time, I swear." She parked at the kitchen table and scribbled, her tongue hanging halfway out of her mouth. She grinned and flipped the notepad over to me. "There!"

The page finally had English words scrawled on it. It looked like a poem of some kind. I had no idea why Nadine was excited until I read the last line. I felt a glimmer of hope. "But what does this mean?" I asked.

"It means we have a chance of waking up your loved ones," Nadine responded, considering the poem thoughtfully. "But I am not sure we can fully eradicate the danger without the other pieces of the puzzle."

I glanced at the paper again, the words searing themselves into my brain. I only understood some of what it said, but if Nadine thought it could help Tony and the others, who was I to doubt her? I nodded. "I'm in. What's first?"

"First, we call your friends and hope they do not have plans tonight." Nadine's eyes sparkled with excitement. "Then I will show you how to use a blade."

Chapter Eighteen

The Champions will awaken and discover the fate
Joining hands with Companions close to the heart
The Dream Walker will dance with the blade of the light
The Burning One sears treachery from arrogance
The Other will heal with acceptance and love
Removing the Peril from the Lives in Oblivion

***

I spent the rest of that morning staring at the words Nadine had written. What did it mean? Obviously I was the Dream Walker it mentioned, and the peril was probably the monster I saw when I'd tried to rescue Tony and the others. But what about the rest of it?

Thinking about it gave me a headache, and I decided to have a run. I was doing a lot of that lately, running. Running in the forest in my other form, running away from the danger and leaving Tony to fend for himself. Yup. I was definitely good at running. I sighed and wrote a note to my mom, telling her where I was going.

I had to be back in an hour anyway, since Nadine thought I needed a crash course in swordplay. She was in the guest room with her computer, watching videos on whatever she could find. I wasn't sure how she thought it would help me, but she was determined to teach me how to swing a sword. She was probably afraid I'd turn tail and run again. And she probably wouldn't be wrong.

It's not like I was prepared for any of this. I'd grown up like any other kid. At least, I thought I had. Looking back, I guess I should've seen the signs. My mom always knew when we were sick, even when we didn't really feel all that yucky. Dad was regularly rebuilding things that seemed fine to me.

I suddenly found myself wishing I had a normal gift like Mom or Dad. I wondered what Tony's gift would be, and I found myself tearing up. What if I couldn't wake him up so he could find out? I wiped my eyes and decided it wasn't going to do Tony any good if I kept scaring myself like this.

I walked out the door and into the bright, warm sunshine. I closed my eyes and bathed in the sunlight for a minute. Colorado weather was unpredictable, but I could usually count on sunshine most days of the year. Even when snow covered the ground, the sun would light up the frozen crystals, making the town sparkle.

Making my way to the forest, I hoped I'd find Leo there so we could run together. His company was enough to make me feel better about things, and I wondered how and when that had happened. I barely knew him, but I was incredibly comfortable around him. I wondered if this was how relationships were supposed to feel. If it was, I definitely wanted it to continue.

I reached the clearing in the woods and looked around, expecting to see Leo pop out between some trees. He didn't. I sighed and took off my shoes, stretched, and shifted. I stretched again, now in my feline form. It felt so different, but so right. I was definitely getting the hang of this shifting thing.

With my claws, I climbed a tall tree and jumped from branch to branch. I was so comfortable up there. I was enjoying myself so much I jumped right past the other cat before I noticed it was there.

Retracing my steps, I wondered if I'd seen a wild animal or a shifter like me. Before I could reach the branch where I'd spotted it, it jumped into my path and hissed. The mountain lion was definitely bigger than me, but it seemed malnourished. Its patchy hair was raised, and its teeth, what it had of them, were long and pointed. If I had time, I could count its ribs. But I didn't have time, because this was definitely not a shifter. It held an attack posture, lowering itself for the pounce.

I hissed back, crouching in the hope it would feel threatened enough to go away. This was supposed to be our woods. Nobody ever said anything about wild animals claiming territory here.

The mountain lion hissed again and bounded off to the right, leaving me to breathe heavily in fear. If it had decided to fight me for the territory, I think it would've won. I had no idea how to fight in this form. I'd never been in a fight in my entire life. Now I regretted not wrestling with Tony. It would at least have helped me be better prepared.

Thinking of Tony made my failures return in a sudden rush. I hurried back to the clearing, keeping an eye out for any more dangerous animals. I didn't run into any, and I was thankful nobody was around to see me weeping hysterically while I put my shoes back on.

I was in full-on post-traumatic panic mode. I could've died back there and then nobody would stand a chance of ever waking up. I wiped away my tears and breathed deeply to calm myself. There was no point in worrying about it now. It was done. I had to look forward. After I saved my brother and teachers, I would worry about learning how to brawl. Until then, I had to focus on the battle ahead and hope that Nadine knew what she was doing. Because I sure as heck didn't.

When I got home, Nadine was sitting on the front porch, sword in hand. I think it was one of those fencing swords. It was long and skinny. I doubted it could do much damage to the thing I'd seen, but what did I know?

"It is about time you showed up. We do not have much time." Nadine stood and shoved a sword at me. She stood with her legs spread wider than her shoulders and pointed her sword up in the air.

"We're going to start now?" I wondered out loud. "We don't have any protective gear or anything. We could get hurt."

Nadine rolled her eyes and shook her sword at me. "En garde, little one. We do not have time for this. Either you learn how to use a sword or you let your brother die. Your choice."

Well, when she put it that way....

I copied her stance and lifted my sword.

I barely had time to take a breath before she was going after me, swinging her blade left and right, up and down. I only had time to react, blocking her swings by pure luck. It took about twenty seconds before she smacked my wounded arm with the side of her sword. "Ow!" I rubbed my injury.

"Hold your sword with one hand, keeping your other arm up to block. Let us try again." She gave me several seconds before attacking again.

We kept this up until I had sweat dripping from my face, into my eyes. My shirt was wet and I swear I'd worn a hole in my shoes.

"You have done well," she finally said, dropping her stance. "Let us take a break. Then we can try again."

I groaned and turned to go inside when I heard a car pull up. I saw a limousine and drew my eyebrows in confusion. *What the-*

Westy stepped out of the back and I groaned again. Homecoming. I'd completely forgotten. I definitely wasn't going, since it didn't even start until after sunset. But I had no clue how I was going to get out of it. The idiot couldn't take a hint if it was seared into a two-by-four that smacked him on the head. I enjoyed that visual for a minute before he reached me. His face was twisted in a mixture of confusion and anger.

"Why aren't you ready? You look disgusting. I can't take you anywhere looking like that. Go change. Be fast about it." He shooed at me and I wondered if this actually worked on girls before. I thought that sadly, it probably had.

"You don't own me, Westy. And you need to stop talking to me like that." I remembered why I'd agreed to go out with him. I felt in my gut that he wasn't involved with all of this. He was a stupid, selfish jerk. He wasn't capable of something like this. But I had to try everything.

One step brought me closer to him, and his expression changed to utter disgust. *I must really stink. Good.* "Tell me what you know about what happened to Tony and the teachers."

Westy smirked and snorted. "They got what they deserved."

I rushed at him so fast he didn't have time to react. My hand closed around his throat, and I saw red. "None of them deserved to be hurt. You'd better not say anything like that ever again. Now," I said, trying to look as scary as possible despite my short stature. "I'll only ask you one more time. Tell me what you know."

He glared at me, clearly angry that a girl was talking back to him for once. "I'm not telling you anything."

That made me mad. Really mad. I felt my teeth poke into my lips. I opened my mouth to snarl. I watched claws grow from my hand, and I knew I'd partially shifted again. Westy's eyes got a panicked look and he made a terrified squeak. "I don't know anything! I swear! Please don't hurt me!" He sobbed and I let him go, willing my hands and face to go back to normal.

"Go away," I said, shooing him to the

curb.

He tripped as he pivoted on his heel and scrambled off to the limo. The tires squealed as it pulled away from the curb. I felt a hand lightly touch my shoulder.

Nadine grinned at me. "You handled that well. I think my work here is done. Let us go inside and get something to eat. You need your strength."

Eating ravenously, I barely stopped to acknowledge Nadine. She took her time, and I wondered if she ate slowly so I didn't feel like a big fat oinker. The more time I spent with her, the cooler she was.

We decided to walk to the woods, shift there, and run the rest of the way to the cave. I had to blow off some more steam, and I don't think she'd shifted for several days. She told me that the cave was definitely the right call, and Mom had set everything up there.

I wondered what Nadine had figured out was missing the last time we did this, but I couldn't think of anything I'd change. I'm sure it had something to do with the text she'd remembered. How she'd remembered something so obscure was a mystery, but I didn't think I'd get that answer any time soon.

When we reached the cave, I could smell all of the different people waiting inside, and I got nervous all over again. Great. I'd have another audience to witness my failures. I took a deep breath, stretched, and shifted.

I walked into the cave and was almost knocked over by Chloe, whose arms wrapped around me in a huge hug. "We can do this, T."

I'm glad she had confidence because I sure didn't. "We? What do you mean?" I pulled back and looked at her, confused.

"Nadine called. She seems to think that we have something to do with helping. She spouted off in another language and said that it meant you needed us. So, here we are." She gestured to my right, and I saw that Vin was there, too.

"Joining hands with Companions close to the heart," I said. "I guess that makes sense. I

don't mean to be a jerk, but you don't have any powers. How are you supposed to be able to help?"

Chloe grinned. "She doesn't think it matters. Something about friendship being stronger than any evil, blah, blah, blah." She shrugged.

The air in the room shifted, and the crowd of people fell silent. It was time. I squared my shoulders and held out my hand to Chloe. She took it and we went to Vin. He took my other hand and we walked to the crystal pedestal, where soft mats had been laid out for us next to the pedestal.

Mom, Dad, and Nadine stood in a line next to the mats. Mom had some electrodes in her hand and when we got close, she stuck them to our temples.

"These will help me monitor you all more closely. We'll do what we can from here, but I'm not sure how much help we'll be." She hugged me tightly and passed me to Dad. A man of few words, he kissed my forehead and squeezed my shoulders before stepping away.

I glanced at the gurneys set up on the other side of the pedestal, and sat on the middle mat. Chloe and Vin sat on either side of me. My hands went out and grasped each of theirs tightly. Chloe's was warm and soft. Vin's was cool and clammy. I squeezed them both for support and closed my eyes. "Here goes nothing."

The darkness felt different this time. I looked around and saw why. Chloe stood to my left, Vin to my right. They were scoping the place.

"This is what you see?" Vin asked. His voice didn't echo, like it should in a big, empty place like this. It stopped almost as soon as it reached me. "How many times have you been here?"

"More times than I'd like," I answered. Standing there felt weird, and I examined my body. I was wearing the same thing I'd been wearing when I was awake, my new purple hoodie and some jeans.

A glimmer of light on the ground caught my eye and I leaned over to look. A pair of swords lay in front of me.

I lifted them to study them more closely. They were both long and dark, with identical markings and cutouts in the blades. I stood and gave them each a practice swing. They felt more natural than the fencing swords Nadine and I had used earlier. Where did they come from? Did it matter? I wanted to save Tony and my teachers, and get out. I didn't want to use these things at all.

I looked beyond Chloe and Vin, and could see figures in the distance. I nodded ahead and started walking. I felt my friends follow me. Our footsteps didn't make a sound. It was eerily quiet.

We reached the figures, who were sitting bent over, like before. I nudged Tony again, knowing it wouldn't do any good. He continued to sit there, unmoving.

"How do we get them out of here?" Chloe asked.

I know it was what we were all thinking. I just wish one of us had an answer.

"Welcome back," a voice said from behind us. We spun around and came face to face with the monster from before. I shoved Chloe and Vin behind me, careful not to stab them with my blades.

"Let us take these people home. I don't want to have to hurt you," I said. I sounded much braver than I felt. My stomach cramped, and I wondered if I could lose my lunch in a dream world.

The creature laughed, a sound that had haunted me since the last time we met. "You're not going anywhere this time. And neither are your friends."

I shifted my body to the proper fighting stance and raised my weapons. "This is your last warning."

The expression on the ever-changing face transformed. The thing was no longer smiling with its many mouths. It began to snarl and crouched to charge at me.

Shifting Dreams

"Look out!" I yelled, hoping my friends could get out of the way before they were trampled. At the last minute, I leaped to my left, rolling and landing behind the monster. Apparently, it was not nearly as agile as I was, and I was happy to have that advantage. My moment of triumph ended quickly when the monster charged again, this time swiping with its talons, barely grazing my sleeve. The fabric ripped and I felt a brief moment of loss.

We did this a few times, lunging and dodging. I had to go on the offense if I was going to get out of this alive. This thing was not going to let me go this time. It showed no signs of getting tired, and my arms already burned with the effort of holding up my blades.

I waited until it finished a charge. Its back was to me when I thrust with my right hand. The sword plunged into the monster's leg.

It let out a howl that ripped at my eardrums. As the wound bled out, a strange thing happened. I watched the leg begin to change. The fur seemed to grow back in on itself, the claws on the feet retracted. The transformation radiated out from the injury site, moving across the creature's hips to the other leg. In about five seconds, both of the massive furry legs had turned into human legs wearing blue jeans and sneakers.

I stared, not sure what was going on. I heard Chloe cry out behind me and searched for her. Beyond her, I saw Tony fading before my eyes. I'd done it. I'd gotten him out of there. That's when I knew what I had to do.

The monster seemed to realize it at the same time, and lunged while my back was turned. I caught the movement out of the corner of my eye, but I wasn't fast enough. It smacked me to the ground, knocking the wind out of my lungs, making me drop my swords. I gasped for breath, trying to stand at the same time.

I felt a searing pain up my back and knew it had clawed me. My spine burned and I turned to face the thing, determined to not let it win. I searched desperately for my blades, growing weaker by the second. I had to do this fast, or I'd never get us out of there.

The creature lunged. I ducked, landing on something cold and sharp. Luck is with me, *I thought, grabbing the sword. I looked around for the other one.*

"Look out!" Vin's yell saved my life.

I jumped to my left, narrowly missing being tackled.

"T! Catch!" Chloe threw my other sword in the air.

I somehow managed to catch the thing by the handle without slicing myself open, and I turned to the monster.

It was now or never. I attacked, managing to slice a thin line into the palm of the monster's furry hand. The hand began change just as the legs had, but I didn't stop to watch. The monster had paused, almost as if it was frozen in place. This was the only chance I had. I took two steps and swung with all my might.

Blood dripped from its neck, the wound closing as the neck changed to a human's. I watched closely, hoping I could figure out who this was. I glanced over at where the teachers had been sitting, and caught the faint shimmer of them fading out of this world. Chloe and Vin were standing next to them, watching them disappear.

When I looked back at where the monster was, I was disappointed, but not terribly surprised to see that he had disappeared as well.

I slumped over in exhaustion and pain. I'd done it. I'd saved three lives. But I still had no idea who the bad guy was, or why he was targeting us. I knew it was a bad GUY though. The blue jeans and t-shirt I'd seen before he faded had given me that much.

I couldn't stand, so Chloe and Vin propped me up on either side.

"How do we get ourselves out of here? Your mom needs to see to you." Chloe couldn't hide her concern.

I tried to smile at her reassuringly. I'm sure it came out more like a grimace. "Just close your eyes," I said before I passed out.

Shifting Dreams

Chapter Nineteen

I opened my eyes to a clamor of noise. Everyone was talking and moving around, pushing to see the people who had woken up from their long, unnatural sleep. I shifted position to look around the cave and the searing pain in my back made me scream.

Mom rushed over to me and touched my face. Her forehead creased with concern and she yelled, "Get out of the way! I need some room here!"

Nobody heard her over the din, except Dad. "EVERYBODY OUT," he boomed. The noise died and people filed out, staring at me with concern on their faces. The whispering began before they'd reached the mouth of the cave, but at least they weren't crowding around me anymore.

"Honey, I need you to breathe deeply and let me turn you over. I need to patch you up," Mom said gently, leaning over me.

Grimacing, I focused on breathing. Funny how such a natural little thing is so hard to do when your body is burning and you're bleeding out. I gasped and cried out when she finally turned me over, but I kept breathing deeply.

I thought I might hyperventilate, but then I felt an oxygen mask slip over my face. Breathing became much easier at that point. It occurred to my muddled brain that maybe oxygen wasn't the only thing swirling through my lungs. I didn't care.

Mom cleaned my back and bandaged my wounds. Luckily, the damage done in the other world was much worse than the damage done here. I heard her say that I would be fine in a few days. I heard the relief in her voice when she said it. I wished I could shift and heal, but at least I had a good doctor.

I nearly cried when I heard Tony's voice from behind me. "Ah, Squirt, what did you get yourself into this time?"

I turned my head to see him propped up on the gurney. He was no longer hooked up to wires, and I felt so relieved. I stuck out my tongue. "Nothing I couldn't handle. Which is more than I can say for you, Loser."

He smiled crookedly at me. "I guess you don't need me to have your back anymore, Tess."

"I always need you at my back, Tony." I grimaced when the last bandage was applied and Mom helped me sit up. Someone grabbed my hand and squeezed.

I smiled at my best friend. "We did it, Chloe. I couldn't have done it without you guys." I reached out to grab Vin's hand and he took it awkwardly. I guess guys don't hold hands unless it's a life or death situation. Oh, well. He could deal with it.

Mom had gone to check out Tony and the others and I heard a slight commotion. When

I looked over, Tony's hospital gown was lifted to his hip and Mom was whispering frantically to one of her nurses.

"What's going on?" I tried to stand up, but my back burned and my head felt light so I dropped back to my previous position.

Mom frowned at me. "I'm not sure, honey. It's probably nothing."

Her expression told me it wasn't *nothing*. I stared at her expectantly. She couldn't start treating me like a kid again, not after what I'd done to save everyone.

I knew she'd come to the same realization when she sighed. "The mark is still here. Tony still has it, as do Jane and Malcolm. I don't know what it means."

I thought about it for a minute, but I had no answers. I knew someone who might, though. "Mom, where's Nadine?"

Mom gestured to the cave entrance and Dad walked out to find her. He came back a minute later, Nadine following behind. She looked excited, her hands fidgeting with each other, her eyes glancing around the cave, taking everything in.

She came to me and looked me over standing back like she was afraid she might catch something by standing too close. "So, it worked. That is wonderful. I cannot wait to hear what happened so I can write it all down." She glanced around, her hands still fidgeting.

"Well, it didn't work completely," I said, feeling like I was totally letting her down.

But she brightened at this. "What about it did not work? You woke everyone up. What else is there?" She looked over at my mom, assuming she had the answers.

Mom didn't disappoint. "The marks on all the victims are still there. Their vital signs are normal, but the marks haven't changed at all."

Nadine rushed over to see what Mom was talking about. She examined the marks for several minutes. Then she nodded. "Mm-hmm."

"What's going on?" I asked from my spot on the ground. I wanted to go over and see the marks they were looking at, but I still felt too light-headed.

Nadine looked at me and frowned. "I thought this might happen. Your work is done for now, but you are still missing pieces of that prophecy."

***

The whole next day, I told Nadine everything that happened while I fought the monster. I went through the story over and over again. She had lots of questions, and I didn't always have the answers. When we got to the part about how I'd released everyone from whatever trance they were in, I told her how the monster had transformed into person piece-by-piece whenever I injured it.

Nadine got excited at this. "It almost seems as though the beast had stolen aspects of each of the animals he had stolen. Your brother disappeared at the same time its legs did, so it must have stolen the speed and strength of his brown bear's lower body. Same with your teachers, the wolverine and the giraffe. I am not entirely sure why it would want a giraffe's neck." She paused, considering. "I suppose while it is not considered dangerous in any way, it is very exotic."

It made sense when she put it that way. I was glad I'd figured it out before I'd become monster kibble. And before anyone else got hurt.

I took a nap and dreamed, but they weren't premonitions anymore. I dreamed about what had happened, in vivid detail. In my dream, I knew it wasn't real anymore, but I had the distinct feeling I was being watched. Like there was someone or something viewing the same event I was. It felt almost like my dream was being probed for my weaknesses. It felt malevolent.

I woke up and had my mom peel off my bandages so I could shower. I felt the need to wash away all of the feelings that my dream had conjured inside me.

When I reached the bathroom, I looked at my back in the mirror. Five long lines ran up the length of my back. They'd already scabbed over, so they were shallow wounds. But I would definitely have a scar. I sighed. It could be worse. I could be dead.

Shivering at this thought, I climbed into the shower. I couldn't make it as hot as I wanted, but the water pulsed on my scalp and relieved the headache I hadn't even felt. When I finally got out, I wrapped myself in my big, fluffy robe and shuffled back to my room.

I opened the door and let out squeak. On my bed sat a sweet, attractive boy.

Leo saw me and instantly stood up and turned his back to me. "Sorry, I didn't know you weren't dressed. I'll uhm...er...wait outside." He headed to my open window and started to climb out.

"Wait," I said. He stopped, but didn't turn around. I had the feeling his cheeks were as red as mine. I hated what I was about to say. "I can't go out with you today, I'm sorry."

His head bobbed back and forth, like he was fighting not to turn around. "Oh, okay. I won't bother you anymore then."

"No, it's not like that," I protested,

chewing on my bottom lip. "Something happened last night and I'm not well enough to go out for a few days. It hurts to move." I laughed at myself.

Leo apparently didn't find it very funny, because his head whipped around and he growled. "Did someone hurt you? Who was it?"

I smiled at his protectiveness. Then, I laughed because he obviously didn't know I could totally take care of myself. I stopped laughing when I realized he wasn't laughing with me. "Sorry, it's kind of complicated."

His face fell. "Okay. Well, see you around."

I didn't want him to walk out of my life forever, but I was wandering into new territory and I didn't know how to handle it. "If you wait for me outside, I'll tell you the story."

With a nod and a grin, he hopped out of my window. I was left standing in my room, hair dripping onto my shoulders. Mom had told me not to recover the wounds, since they'd already scabbed, so I picked out a loose-fitting shirt with a camisole underneath. Getting dressed was one of the hardest things I'd ever done. My back was tight and stretched uncomfortably whenever I moved my arms, and I knew I'd made the right decision in not going out with Leo.

I stared at the mirror when I was done, wishing I could do something pretty and elaborate with my hair. There was no way I could keep my arms up that long, though. I sighed and combed through the dark strands, flipping my head over to give it some volume. Last, a layer of mascara and some lip gloss. Just because I felt like poop didn't mean I should look like it. I took one last look in the mirror and decided this was the best I was going to get today.

I turned to the window, ready to climb out, and paused. I'd had enough of sneaking around. If my parents had a problem with Leo, they'd have to deal with it. I wasn't going to miss out on this great guy because my parents were prejudiced against wolf-shifters.

Taking a deep breath, I opened my door

and walked down the stairs. Dad was sitting in the kitchen, reading.

"Dad, Leo is here and I'm going to go outside and talk to him," I said. I waited what seemed like an hour, but it was probably less than a minute while Dad stared me down.

"Okay, honey. Stay close and don't irritate your injuries," he said. He looked back at his newspaper. "Let me know if you guys need anything."

I held in a celebratory yell and instead calmly said, "Thanks. We will."

When I walked out the front door, I felt like I'd gotten older. Matured. The fights and the rescue and everything else that had happened to me recently hadn't made me feel all that special. That short conversation with Dad was the thing that made me feel like I was no longer a kid. It was awesome.

I grinned at Leo when I saw him, and we sat on the grass and talked. He was concerned about everything that had happened, and I assured him I was fine. He held my hand

and my arm went all tingly. I knew Dad was keeping watch, so I kept things light.

I was happy, though. I saved my brother and teachers, survived a battle with an unspeakable creature, and got the boy. I didn't think there was much more I could ask for...except maybe another kiss. Before he left, Leo leaned in and softly brushed his lips across my cheek. It would do for now.

***

I over-estimated the girl. I hadn't wanted to hurt anyone, until she came along. Why did she always have to ruin everything?

I would have to keep my experiments on the down-low. I can't keep my subjects indefinitely anymore. I'll have to Steal their Dreams and give them back in the morning. At least, until I get this thing handled.

Yeah, people are gonna pay for how they treated me.

Soon....

Made in the USA
Charleston, SC
16 June 2014